Anne Ber

A Rainbow
Murder Mystery

Praise for *False Promises*—

"Sandra Robson has managed the best Florida can provide: a taste of the surf and a murder set among the ranches and small towns of rural Florida. Hooray for a savvy sleuth and a cast of characters who sometimes aid in tracking down the killer and sometimes appear to be the guilty party. Twists and turns aplenty, you'll never guess the outcome until the end."

—Lesley A. Diehl, author of
the Eve Apple Mysteries,
the Big Lake Murder Mysteries and
the Laura Murphy Mysteries

"Photo-journalist Keegan Shaw has baggage. Married, divorced, a dead ex-husband, she's solved two murders and she's dating an English rocker. And the eccentric cast of characters she's surrounded by have even crazier lives. False Promises is a locked room suspense/murder that will have you guessing right up to the end. Wonderful story, strong characters, highly recommended."

—Don Bruns, author of
the Quentin Archer Series,
the Stuff Series and
the Caribbean Series

To Anne,
Enjoy!
Sandy Robson

False Promises

A Keegan Shaw Mystery

SANDRA J. ROBSON

Rainbow Books, Inc.
FLORIDA

False Promises: A Keegan Shaw Mystery

Author's Website: SandraRobson.com
Softcover ISBN 978-1-56825-193-6
ePub ISBN 978-1-56825-194-3

Published by
Rainbow Books, Inc.
P. O. Box 430
Highland City, FL 33846-0430
Telephone (863) 648-4420
Facsimile (863) 647-5951
RBIbooks@aol.com • RainbowBooksInc.com

Individuals' Orders
Toll-free (800) 431-1579
BookCH.com • Amazon.com • AllBookStores.com

Front cover image by iStockPhoto
Author photo on the back cover by Hobie Hiler

Written, produced and printed in the United States of America.

Dedicated to the ageless and beautiful Santuario de Chimayo
in New Mexico, home of the miraculous healing earth.

Other Books by Sandra J. Robson

Mystery Fiction

False Impression: A Keegan Shaw Mystery

False as the Day Is Long: A Keegan Shaw Mystery

Self-Help

Girls' Night Out: Changing Your Life One Week at a Time

Acknowledgments

Thanks to

Stephen Leighton and retired police captain Lloyd Jones for tutorials on police procedures, scene-of-crime and interrogation techniques.

Greenridge Stables for letting me hang around the barns and talk to their horses and cats.

The real Lee Lee, who lent her name and background to this story.

To Father Mike, who never was.

And to my husband Bill, who drove me all over Florida to visit old and historic churches. Oh yeah, and who always offers to help me with the sex scenes.

False Promises

Prologue

November, 1999
Lost River, Florida

Murder and miracles don't mix. Or at least they shouldn't. And Lost River's miracle was a simple, heartwarming story, the absolute antithesis of bloodshed. It began when Andreas, a seven-year-old Guatemalan mute, helped his stepfather dig up a cracked floor at St. Jude's Catholic Church. The floor, in a storage room at the back of the church, had never been anything but unpainted concrete, and beneath it was virgin soil, so to speak. As the man hauled the jagged pieces of cement outside, the boy ran his dump truck in the exposed dirt, creating miniature mountains of dank earth. When his stepfather returned, Andreas lifted a fistful of dirt and spoke the first word he had ever uttered.

"Cold."

Under ordinary circumstances, this curious incident might have generated mild interest. But its timing — the eve of the millennium — caught the attention of a local reporter with big dreams and a preference for two inch print.

Mute No More! Boy Says Earth Helped Him Speak!

Readers who'd grown tired of murder, mayhem and general ungodliness, warmed to the headlines. Local newspapers front-paged the story for two precious days before it spread to area TV stations, the national papers, network and cable news, and the tabloids.

The chaos that followed was a shock for the inhabitants of Lost River. Seekers after healing, knowledge, truth, or all of the above, arrived in such staggering numbers the governor had to call out the state militia to patrol the streets and stop strangers from pitching their sleeping bags in local yards. Tour buses added St. Jude's to their theme park itinerary, and bright blue Porta-Potties became permanent fixtures across the street from the church. Twenty thousand people showed up in the weeks surrounding the millennium.

Neither *60 Minutes* nor *The Oprah Winfrey Show* succeeded in securing an interview. Andreas' stepfather kept the miracle boy from the press and limited himself to "It was the hand of God," no matter how the question was phrased or rephrased. Andreas' mother, who spoke only Kanjobal, cried and wrung her hands through an interpreter. Father Mike, the Catholic priest, was so appalled, he refused to speak to anyone.

In the years that followed, residents endured the nonstop disruption of their lives. Eventually, the number of visitors began to decline and St. Jude's returned to modified pre-miracle status. Lost River settled into its notoriety without abandoning its small town feel and took pride in being a secondary Mecca for those in search of healing.

And then, after all the dust had literally settled, a dedicated, muckraking snake arrived in the garden. A man with a soul above magic dirt who was destined to end up dead on a pile of it. A man for whom yours truly, Keegan Shaw, had somehow managed to become responsible.

Chapter 1

For Florida surfers, nothing beats the combination of wind and waves following a storm. There's something addictive about paddling out to the biggest rollers the east coast ever gets, balancing on an unstable piece of wood for six seconds, and being engulfed by cold ocean. Still, after two hours of paddling and balancing, even the thrill of four-foot swells gets edged out by the reality of a heavy wet suit and sixty-eight-degree weather.

I stood ankle deep in sea foam, catching my breath and watching a huge wave form a couple of hundred yards out. I was done for the day, tapped out, but this wave was something else. It rolled to a peak, formed a perfect blue-green tunnel and crashed like a broken tumbler of curaçao, flinging foamy breakers toward the shore. Simply spectacular.

Now, what was it about surfing that always reminded me of

Tom Roddler? The high that came from riding a cresting wave? The pounding surf? The sense of satisfaction when it was over? A smile worked its way across my face before I could stop it. Tom had started calling me again, leaving suggestions that we have a drink and catch up. So far, I had sent the calls straight to trash. Tom was good with words — too good. He could talk a starving widow out of her last scrap of bread without breaking a sweat.

I trudged through soft sand, board tucked under my arm, reminding myself again why Tom Roddler and I hadn't worked out. The list was lengthy: too old for me, a serial dater, a politician, too high profile, unreliable, et cetera, et cetera. Unfortunately, Tom reminded me of my hero, Leroy Jethro Gibbs. You know, the guy on *NCIS*? And because of that, I held on longer than I should have, waiting for Tom's compassion and integrity chips to activate. They never did, of course. Surprise, surprise.

Anyway, I had written Tom off completely after I met Reid, a former English rocker, six years younger than me, who ran an art gallery in London. I'm not crazy about long distance relationships, but so far we'd managed to meet often enough to keep the buzz alive. And Reid did have integrity, although I wasn't sure about compassion. More important, in less than a month he'd be in Seminole Beach for Christmas. That thought kept me smiling all the way to the car.

My aging BMW was one of only three vehicles in the parking area. I fished the car keys out of a waterproof pocket and popped the trunk. Then I leaned the surfboard against a fender and started shedding wet suit. Just as I reached for a pair of warm, dry jeans, my cell phone pinged.

It was Tom; I knew it without looking.

But it wasn't. The number displayed wasn't one I recognized.

Probably some politician's aide leaving scary, random messages about his opponent's plan for Medicare. Not that it meant anything to me; I was still twenty-plus years away from government health. I dragged on the jeans with one hand and thumbed *talk* with the other.

"Keegan? It's Maggie," said a tentative voice on the other end.

"Maggie?" I mashed the cell between my face and shoulder and tried to pull a thick sweatshirt over my head. "Maggie! What's going on?"

I hadn't actually seen Maggie Gilchrist since I'd worked as a photojournalist in England in the nineties. We'd been good friends, best friends really, but we lost touch when I came back to the U.S.. I lost touch with everybody when I moved to Florida. You do that when you marry a practicing alcoholic and you're the last one to know.

The phone slipped and I snatched it back.

". . . been thinking a lot about you," Maggie was saying, "since I met Amy in New York . . . Oh, hell, Keegan. The truth is, I need a favor. A big favor."

Amy.

My lips pressed together in a flat line. Anytime Amy was involved, life had a way of getting complicated. True, all she'd done this time was fly to NYC to promote her cookbook. But while there, she'd sloshed down a lot of champagne at a Food Network party and exchanged life stories with an assistant editor called Maggie Gilchrist. Eventually, they realized that the Keegan Shaw Amy roomed with in Seminole Beach was the same one Maggie had known in London years ago. Amy immediately called me, and Maggie and I connected after more than a decade. Now, two months later, Maggie was calling me again.

I rubbed my wet hair with a towel, trying to imagine what kind of favor Maggie wanted after all this time.

"Keegan," the tentative voice was back, "do you remember Stubb? Stubb Flanders?"

I stopped rubbing. Now there was a name permanently etched in my brain. Except he'd been christened Stewart, if I remembered correctly. *Stubb* was his own personal conceit.

"Sure, I remember. Haven't thought of him in years."

There was a little silence. "Well, he's . . . he's in Florida — not far from you, actually. In a place called Lost River — maybe twenty minutes away?"

"Really?" The Stubb I remembered was strictly a city boy from the East End of London. The idea of him spending quality time in an agricultural, mostly cow town, seemed unlikely at best. "What's he doing there?"

"Well, I got him . . . er, he's doing a story on the miracle earth . . ."

"The what? Oh, the St. Jude's Church thing?"

"Right. He went down there a couple of weeks ago, and he's called a few times. From the local pub . . ."

I nodded to myself. That was the Stubb I remembered.

". . . but he's gotten off track, I guess. He's supposed to be writing an article about the people who come looking for a miracle. Stubb can write, you know. It isn't his favorite thing, but he's good when he puts his mind to it. It's just, uh, he's getting more and more out of touch. Keeps talking of exposing scams and that sort of thing. Well, I was wondering if you could just go out there . . . see, uh, how he's doing, find out how much he's actually written. I'm coming down myself in a week or so, but . . ."

"Where's he staying?"

"Not actually sure. Some motel, I think. If you could just find him, look after him for a bit, Keegan. I'm . . . well, I'm afraid he'll mess this up, and he could stand some good press for a change . . ."

I drank coffee straight from the thermos and thought about it. When you took all the "uhs" and "ers" and "wells" out of Maggie's account, it was clear Stubb Flanders was ass over elbows in trouble again. Why she cared after all these years was a mystery, but I owed Maggie. Enough that I couldn't refuse her request. And, unless Stubb had changed drastically, it was simply a question of finding which bar in Lost River had become his temporary home, then keeping an eye on him for a few days. How hard could that be?

Which is how I made the fourth worst decision in my life.

Chapter 2

Bad decisions aren't exactly rarities in my day-to-day existence, but only a few have been real zingers. Like the one when I married the alcoholic. And the one when I moved into the house he left me in the divorce settlement and ended up with a bunch of artists as tenants.

But even before those life-altering choices, there was one decision I spent years trying to forget. And during the emotional tsunami that followed it, Maggie Gilchrist had literally saved my life. It was now payback time. Short of feeding Stubb with a spoon or changing his diapers, she could count on me.

It was nearly eight when I drove out to Lost River to look for Stubb Flanders, and it took almost two hours to track him down. Which was ridiculous since the entire population of Lost

River totals fewer than 4,000, and 3,000 of them were home watching *Dancing With the Stars*.

In the process of canvassing all the possible places Mr. Flanders might be hanging out, I gathered a good bit of information. None of it was info I was going to enjoy passing on to Maggie. "The Guy with the Cameras" had not been low profile during his two weeks in town. Nearly everyone had heard about him and none of the things they had to say were good.

Lost River has only two main streets: Center, also known as State Road 605, and Canal Point. It has a marina, a supermarket, two Hispanic groceries, convenience stores, an eighty-year-old hotel, a Catholic church and a water-damaged post office. But it makes up in nightlife what it lacks in general amenities. There are at least five bars on the main drag, three more on Canal Point and a handful of others off unlit, unpaved side roads.

I found Stubb in the least hygienic dive of all, a chipped-pink cinder block building with bars on the windows and the smell of old beer on the floor. I didn't have any trouble recognizing him, even after twelve years. For one thing, he was the only guy in the place who spoke English — as opposed to American — and he had two cameras slung around his neck.

You made a mistake if you took him at face value: the dark hair falling over his forehead, begging to be re-arranged; the eyes a little narrowed as if he was always looking into the sun; the smile that said you should be having as great a time as he was. The truth was, Stubb was a boozer, a womanizer and a user, pretty much in that order. His only redeeming qualities were his absolute brilliance for getting the right picture and his ability to spot a scam.

He was now watching a farmer and a cowboy shoot pool on a table with a felt top that was only a memory, but he wasn't watching as much as he was playing Drink and Bait 'Em. Stubb had clearly been studying Simon Cowell and decided that verbal abuse was the key to winning back his once-adoring public. Along with pointed remarks about the pool player's expertise, eyesight and female antecedents, Stubb was bemoaning Lost River's mind-boggling lack of culture: "No theater, no library, no *cinema*, for God's sake."

The dive was called the Whole Hog Saloon and had only one entrance. I sat at the empty end of the bar, and a waitress in faux-lizard boots got the beer I requested. I drank it down fairly quickly and kept an eye on the down-and-dusty crowd, mostly cowboys and field-workers, but nobody paid much attention to me. They were all pretending not to listen to Stubb, who was tossing out English idioms and laying on a Cockney accent with a palette knife. Between remarks about the town's cultural deficiencies, he lectured on religious superstition and a psychotic disorder called elective mutism.

"That's what this whole miracle thing is about, really; little buggers refusing to talk because they're anal retentive. The kid's mental, of course. They all are. They can talk if they want.

"But what I really can't understand," Stubb continued, rolling up the sleeves of his chambray shirt, "is how the dirt stays the same level. Every day, people carry it away by the bagful, but the next morning there's always plenty for the new crowd. What's betting if I parked my backside in the churchyard one night, I'd catch the local priest lugging in a plackie bag full of miracle earth?"

"What the fuck difference it make if it's blessed?" growled the cowboy, a short, square man who'd obviously had a bellyful of English photographers.

Stubb gave him a big, toothy smile. "The difference is . . .

people've been taking it away for years, thousands of bags of dirt, yet it never runs low. The brochure says so. If that's not true and they're just hauling it in by the truckload, then it's a lie. Lies are hoaxes, not miracles. Can't say fairer than that, can I?"

The bartender wiped her hands across the seat of her ripped cutoffs and drew me a second beer without asking. She pulled her long dark hair into a ponytail and tilted her head in Stubb's direction. "He a friend of yours?"

I grinned at her. "Not even a little."

"That's good. You won't have to scrape him up off the floor. What's a plakkie bawg?"

"British for plastic bag."

She rolled her eyes. "He don't always have a accent. He really English?"

I nodded. "But he lived in the U.S. awhile."

She shook her head and started back down the bar. "He oughta git."

She was right. The locals were growing more hostile with every drink, and the short cowboy was belligerent as he recited cures he had witnessed firsthand.

"Oh, stuff it, Harry." The other pool player, the farmer, threw down his cue. "He don' care, and dirt don' cure nothing, 'cluding the economy. Ask Porky Joe over there. He's been rolling in magic dirt for months." He gestured across the room at three guys sitting at a corner table. They were all dressed in grubby shorts and T-shirts, all deeply tanned. The one with longish black hair looked around briefly and shrugged. The second, oblivious, drained his glass of beer. The third was face down on the table.

"How many times you took the dirt cure?" the farmer said, laughing. He seemed to be addressing the face-down guy. "Ten?

Twelve? Shit." He made three syllables out of the last word and ambled out of the bar.

Stubb had swiveled around and was staring at the three men in the corner. "Which one didn't get cured?" he demanded, his words slurring a little.

"Drunks don't cure," the cowboy snapped, thumping his pool cue in the palm of his other hand, "but I know people who're healthy as hell because of St. Jude's dirt. We don't need no English asshole telling us our business."

I stood up and abandoned my beer. As much as I'd enjoy it, Maggie was going to be upset if Stubb got the crap beat out of him five minutes after I found him. But how to get him out of the bar in one piece?

Blue-eyed female stupidity seemed like the best bet. I flipped blonde hair behind my ears and called, "Time to go, lots to do tomorrow," in a cutesy, breathy voice, as I crossed the uneven wood floor to the pool table. "It's Keegan, Stubb," I said in a low voice, "Keegan Shaw."

He turned around with a cheeky smile, which got wider when he saw me. "Keegan Shaw. My god, it is. You haven't changed at all." He draped an arm around my shoulders. "Still a gorgeous bird. What are you doing in Florida? Let's go somewhere and . . . talk." He pulled a twenty pound note out of his shirt pocket, squinted his eyes to look at it then put it back. "Can you get my tab, love? I seem to be short Americano dinero."

The bartender took my money with a look that said I was a bigger fool than she had supposed and said under her breath, "Don't hang around outside."

I waved away the change, snaked an arm around Stubb's waist and headed for the front door. Outside, I steered us down the wide dirt path that doubled for a street to my car. Stubb leaned heavily against me. He was certainly one over the eight, as his British friends would have said. If he actually had any left.

I ignored his suggestion that, first, he drive and, second, we should both get in the back seat for awhile and shoved him in on the passenger side.

"Where are you staying? I'll drive you home."

He waved an airy hand. "Oh, here and there. Why don't we see if we can find a warm bed somewhere and discuss old times. What are you doing in this dump, anyway?"

I almost tossed him on the street and drove away. Almost. But I had promised Maggie I'd help. As I shut the passenger door, I could hear voices, at least two, somewhere behind us, and they didn't sound particularly friendly. I slammed my own door and blew out of town as fast as my aging BMW could go.

The streets were empty and no lights followed us, but I was still uneasy. Only when we crossed the long bridge without incident and turned off on the main highway did I begin to breathe normally. My headlights swept a tangle of weeds, and we flew down two dark lanes flanked by citrus groves, stands of pine, and palm trees. It was like the back of beyond — no moon, no stars, no streetlights. Nothing but scrub, the occasional battered mobile home and endless black sky.

"Maggie called," I said to Stubb. "She said you were writing a story about St. Jude's magic earth. She's worried about you."

"Maggie worries, it's what she does," he said in a colorless voice. "I got busy at the church and forgot to call for a few days. I was working tonight, in fact, but the stupid priest put the alarm on early and I had to get out. He got all Bolshie when he saw me checking out the alarm keypad."

I glanced sideways at him. "Maybe he thought you were trying to disable it."

"I was." Stubb laughed, pulled out a hip flask and fiddled with the screw top. "The really stupid thing — the thing I can't figure out — is why an alarm at all? There's not a fucking thing in the whole church worth shit. Even the statues are just wood with gold paint."

"As I remember," I said, wondering how much he'd actually had to drink, "some cult group got into the church and camped out for a few days when the miracle thing first happened. It was cheaper to put in an alarm system than it was to hire a guard to keep the nutsos out. It was in all the papers at the time."

"Yeah, well, I doubt that story. More likely there's something valuable hidden there. Something nobody knows anything about. Hidden by that priest . . ."

I rolled my eyes in the dark. I had forgotten Stubb's predilection for conspiracy theories. Once he got started, it was impossible to shut him up.

But this time he let it go, slid over to my side of the car and offered me the flask. "Pull off the road. Let's 'ave a drink." His speech was becoming seriously muddled.

"Can't. No time."

"Plenty of time. Seize the moment! Who said that? Anyway, be a good girl and pull over." I could hear the smile in his voice. "I can make you see God."

"Sorry." I kept my eyes on the road. "Not into threesomes this week."

That stopped him for half a second, then, "Maggie sent you after me, didn't she? If you're worried about her, don't. What the eyes don't see, the heart can't grieve." He reached out and took a firm hold on my right boob.

I swatted his hand away, just as a gigantic spotlight flashed on behind us, lighting up the inside of the car like high noon.

Almost immediately, a monster pick-up truck came roaring out of nowhere, passed us in the left lane and swung back over in front of me. Its tires were taller than my hood. The blinding spotlight, eerily disembodied, stayed directly behind us.

Stubb twisted around in his seat, got a face-full of glare and swore. "What the bloody hell is that?"

"Either extraterrestrials or somebody you pissed off at the bar." I tromped the accelerator to the floor, but the BMW only goes about eighty-five, and only that when it feels like it. The whole vehicle began to shudder.

Whatever was behind us kept pace easily, and the brilliant light was unnerving. The truck in front of me swerved into the left lane and back into the right a couple of times, then threw on its brakes.

Stubb turned around and gave the spotlight what the Brits call "two fingers" and we call one.

I stood on my own brakes and the BMW slid sideways. "You better hope they don't —"

The sound of a shot rang out, and my rear window shattered. I heard rather than saw the shards of glass showering the back seat.

"Get down!" I screamed at Stubb, "Some jerk's got a gun!"

"Not to worry!" he shouted back.

Which was when I realized he was the jerk who'd shot out my window.

He stuck his arm between the bucket seats, fired again, and the giant spotlight disappeared, leaving us in total, mind-numbing darkness.

I gripped the wheel hard until my eyes adjusted, aimed for the middle of the road and tried not to end up in the ditch. The pick-up in front of us must have accelerated right off the map;

one minute it was there, the next there was nothing but a long stretch of two lane highway, illuminated solely by my headlights.

"No fat ass cowboy's going to run me off the road!" Stubb bellowed. "I've been places they can't imagine, seen things they couldn't —"

"Yeah, yeah. Where's the other truck?" I demanded in a shaky voice. "Still behind us? They're not going to ram us, are they?"

"I don't see any headlights."

"They didn't have any headlights when they caught us up, Stubb. They were driving dark on purpose."

"Yeah, well, I took care of that. They're gone now."

I had zero faith in Stubb's ability to take care of anything, but the BMW was eating up the road back to Seminole Beach, and I didn't waste time arguing. No monster trucks showed up in the next three miles. By the time we passed Jimmy's Trailer Camp and were under the street lights lining the turnpike entrance, it was clear we weren't being chased anymore.

"Where'd you get a gun? My God, if you kill somebody, I'll be an accessory."

"Never mind. Forget it." From his tone, Stubb was sobering up, which was good because he'd probably stop trying to feel me up.

However, the gods gave me a genuine reprieve. Stubb unscrewed the top of his pocket flask, swallowed at least half of whatever was in it and passed out a couple of minutes later, still holding onto his gun.

I glanced over at him and started to laugh — helpless laughter just edged with hysteria. Stubb's weapon looked like a toy. It was certainly toy-sized, bright pink and silver with a black rubber grip. Where the hell had he got it? And how had he managed to hit anything with it?

The house was dark when I pulled up out front; my roomers were apparently having an early night. I was going to need help extracting Stubb from the passenger seat, which meant climbing two flights of stairs and rousing Bear out of the sleeping bag he inhabits on his bedroom floor.

Tonight he was inhabiting it alone, but generally he shares with Amy, our cook. I shook his shoulder twice, which had no effect at all. But when I mentioned the word *gun*, he rolled out and followed me downstairs, pulling on a pair of jeans as he went. Bear sleeps nude.

Bear also runs, works out, kayaks and surfs, so he hauled Stubb out of the car and slung him across his back without much effort, although he did a double take when he saw my rear window.

I retrieved the pink handgun and Stubb's hip flask, took them around the side of the house and stuck them in what was left of Jesse's kitchen garden, kicking a little dirt over both items as a precaution. By the time I got up to the second floor and Room Number Four, where I'd told Bear to put him, Stubb was face down on the hardwood floor.

"Leave him there. He'll just throw up in the bed," Bear said, waving away whiskey fumes. "Who is he, anyway, and why the hell'd you bring him home?"

"He's a friend of Maggie's. I promised to babysit him for a few days."

Bear made a face. He didn't like Maggie on principle, even though he'd never met her. It reminded him of the two horniest months of his life when Amy, his significant other, was in New York promoting her cookbook.

"Maggie's all right," I assured Bear, "and she'll be here by the weekend. Probably stay at a motel out by the interstate. That's the last we'll see of him."

"Good." Bear yawned and went out into the hall. "Looks like a card-carrying member of A.A. to me."

"Alcoholics Anonymous?"

"No, Assholes Anonymous. What'd you do with the gun, anyway? More important, what was he doing with it?"

I told him about the trucks following us home, and he made a disgusted sound in his throat.

"I'll vacuum the mess out of your car tomorrow morning. But if I was him, I wouldn't go back to Lost River 'less I was in a body bag." He started up the stairs, then turned and looked back at me. "You okay?"

"Certainly. I was more afraid of the guy in my car than the guys following us."

Bear continued up to his room, and I went down half a flight to the mezzanine, my tiny apartment between first and second floors. The mezzanine consists of a miniscule kitchen and bath, a slightly larger bedroom, a closed-in porch and a landing that doubles as a sitting room, which means two wicker armchairs and a lamp. The chairs overlook a twisting flight of stairs down to the kitchen and a short flight leading out to the main staircase.

Under the hottest water I could stand, I showered away memories of the Whole Hog Saloon and the creepiness of playing reverse chicken with monster pick-ups. Then, in spite of the late hour, I called New York.

Maggie picked up halfway through the first ring.

"Stubb?"

"Nope, it's Keegan. Listen, I found him. He's here, asleep, but I think you'd better come down now. Don't wait 'til next week."

Her sigh came out in a puff of breath. "What's the matter?

I told her about being chased out of Lost River and Stubb's

gunplay. "We were lucky tonight, but he's only been here two weeks, and I think everybody in town wants to kill him."

"What on earth has he done?"

"Well, first, he apparently hits on every woman who crosses his path. Second, his people skills suck. While I was looking around town for him, I heard a dozen stories: He had Andreas, the miracle-earth boy who's now twenty-something, screaming and making devil horns on his forehead two minutes into the interview. Andreas's stepfather thought Stubb was godless and threatened to shoot him. The girl who helps clean the church claimed Stubb asked her out for a 'talk,' spiked her drink and seduced her. *Her* father wants to shoot him too."

I took a breath, heard no response, and continued. "He apparently got pushy with a lady rancher about the church's miracle earth brochure and she ran him off her property with a loaded shotgun. That's just some of the local gossip. He also tried to smuggle a cell phone into St. Jude's to take pictures, so the priest had to post a guard. Shall I go on?"

Silence.

"Anyway, now he haunts the church, checking the dirt levels with a measuring tape and posting them on his blog along with remarks just short of actionable."

There was another silence that told me Maggie had seen Stubb's blog.

"Sorry I got you involved in this, Keegan. Nothing ever changes, does it?" She let out a sigh that was almost a whimper. "Okay, all right. I'll get a plane out tomorrow, but it'll probably be evening. Just don't let him out on his own 'til I get there. Encourage him to work, if possible. Oh, and I gave him a cell phone. Make sure he keeps it charged. Please. Just one more day."

I said okay, rang off and crawled into bed. Tomorrow Maggie would arrive, take Stubb off my hands and that would be the end of that.

Chapter 3

Relief over Maggie's imminent arrival didn't extend to a good night's sleep. I drifted from one bizarre dream to another, none of them, oddly enough, featuring pickups, cowboys or guns. Most were distorted memories of the years when Maggie Gilchrist and I were considerably younger and working in London — the years when we rolled out of bed without makeup, traveled long distances by plane and train without getting tired, and our biggest concern was capturing the picture no one else would ever see.

When I finally woke up for good, it was nearly nine, and the world seemed an older, more depressing place. I pulled on some clothes and went down to the kitchen, thinking about the Stubb Flanders who'd been such a hot number at *Deceptions* magazine all those years ago.

The kitchen was deserted, except for Amy, who was wearing workout clothes and running shoes. About once a week, Amy decides she needs to lose weight, drives to the gym and does twenty miles on the stationary bike. Then she comes home and makes pastry.

"Who's in Number Four?" she said, the minute I walked through the door.

I filled one of her French coffee bowls with Kona and warm, foamy milk and told her about my trip to Lost River.

"Whew! Was he just drunk or is he a total screw-up?" She pulled on an oven mitt and levered a heavy baking pan out of the oven. Amy is Italian on her father's side and Irish on her mother's. Her Italian side has been in the restaurant business since Julius Caesar decided to feed his army something besides beef jerky. Her Irish side suffers fools seldom, if at all. She has short, shiny, dark hair, carries fifteen extra pounds and never lies. She won't let you lie, either, even to yourself.

She transferred croissants from the pan to a platter with a pair of tongs, shook off the oven mitt and gave me an assessing look.

"How do you know this Stubb guy, anyway? You sure he's really Maggie's boyfriend and not some long lost love of yours . . . from the bad old days?"

"Positive." I helped myself to a fat, flaky croissant and slathered on butter. "Maggie and I were working for a magazine called Concepts when she fell for Stubb. He was chief photographer for a rival publication, Deceptions, but most people thought he was just big talk."

"No," Amy muttered from the stove, "imagine that."

"Actually, he wasn't. In a little over a year, he exposed three major frauds: a counterfeit Picasso in a Scottish castle, fake UFOs in Iceland and a ghost buster at a Rhode Island mansion who was using phony thermal imaging equipment. His reputation — and his ego — went right over the top."

I took a couple of mouthfuls of coffee and felt energy flow through my veins in the direction of my brain. Blessed caffeine, my drug of choice.

"Maggie was young, but she was a talented, feisty, career girl," I went on. "a true Scorpio who always got even, whether it took ten minutes or ten years. She should have been immune to the Stubbs in the world, but she wasn't. The more press he got, the more she worried he was slipping away from her. Which was a huge joke; everybody knew he'd slipped away in at least three major European capitals."

"So she dumped him?" Amy said with a grin.

"Nope. He disappeared into a Bolivian jungle on some secret assignment, there was a big scandal, people got killed, and everybody blamed him. He moved to the U.S. to hide out, but I don't think he's worked in years."

Amy was shaking her head. "She never even mentioned him when I was in New York. Why would she have anything to do with him now, let alone help him?"

I shrugged. "Compassion? Love? Stupidity? She thinks he needs a good assignment to get his confidence back, but she's worried about the way he's doing it. I promised to babysit him until she can get down here and do it herself."

"And you agreed to do this because . . ."

I shrugged again. "I owe Maggie."

"Must owe her big time."

I started to say something, then stopped as I heard footsteps on the stairs.

Stubb Flanders shambled into the kitchen, face wrinkled from too many late nights bellying up to the bar.

"Sorry, I was an awful berk last night," he muttered with such good-natured sincerity, I almost believed him. "Shouldn't match drinks with cowboys. Not very clever."

He gave Amy a wry smile. "I'm Stubb Flanders — your new house guest, apparently. Keegan and I go back a long way." He shifted the smile to me, intact. "Enlighten me, please. I remember a rather wicked car chase, some heavy-duty floodlights and several uncongenial rednecks. Was there more?"

"Not much," I said, shrugging. "I promised Maggie I'd find you and bring you here for a few days. Some of your friends in Lost River . . . objected."

I waited for him to mention the gun, but he didn't. Instead, he sat down carefully at the table and said to Amy, in an exhausted voice, "Do you think I could have some coffee?"

"Sure." Her dark eyes sparkled as she pointed to the coffee maker on the counter.

After a second, he got up, shuffled over and made a production out of pouring his own. "Any chance of a sticky bun?" he said hopefully, eyeing the tray of croissants.

"Nope." Amy is only moved by wistfulness if you're six years old.

Stubb sighed, pushed dark hair back off his forehead and took a croissant, which he proceeded to dismember and stuff in his mouth. When it was gone, he drank more coffee, yawned and looked over at me. "How long have you lived in Florida? And where am I, by the way?"

"Seminole Beach. My house. A few miles from Lost River."

"Ah." He nodded. "I saw it on the map, but I've been too busy to explore the coast. How about showing me around town, having a drink somewhere? As I remember, we never actually spent much time together in the old days." The smile he gave me was all charm. "Besides, I owe you one for saving me from," the smile widened, "a likely beating. Probably best to avoid Lost River for a few days. And it never hurts to chill, right?"

"Sure." I watched as he started on a second croissant. "Oh, by the way, Maggie's flying in tonight. She decided not to wait 'til next week."

The kitchen was silent as Stubb allowed the words to register, and I was reminded of one of those kids' toys called Transformers. One second it's a family car, the next it's a ninja fighter. In the silence, he shifted from laid-back, regular guy, intent on quality down time, to working professional, albeit one with an obvious hangover.

"Well, then." He sat where he was, staring at the far wall. "Okay, then. No time for leisure; it'll have to be tonight."

He flashed me a calculating look. "Since Maggie talked you into helping me, I assume I can count on you for assistance."

"Something like that. What do you have planned?"

"I'll keep that to myself, thanks very much, but it means a trip to Lost River tonight. And I'll need some equipment. A folding chair, bug spray. Some thermoses of coffee."

When I didn't say anything, he glanced at his watch. "And you best get a move on, love. My assistants are supposed to make life easier for me, not sit around all day noshing."

Amy's head popped around. There was a just-before-the-storm lull as she waited to see if I was going to take a chunk out of someplace that would significantly increase his pain level, but I couldn't be bothered. Maggie would be here by nine p.m., ten latest, and Stubb would no longer be my responsibility.

Stubb frowned and brushed dark hair out of his eyes. "And I'm not going back to that redneck hole in the ground without some kind of protection," he informed me. "What happened to my gun?"

"I thought you had it."

He got up and went out, letting the back door swing shut behind him.

Amy pulled back the kitchen curtain. "He's going through your car," she said after a moment.

"Really? I hope he doesn't cut his jugular vein on the back window."

Amy leaned back against the sink and regarded me thoughtfully. "He's not actually that bad, Keegan. Italian men can be much worse. He at least seems salvageable."

I gave her a look. "Add your name to the long list of disillusioned woman who believed that."

She reached for her own cup of coffee. "Are you really going to drive him back out there tonight?"

"Why not? It'll get him out of the house. When Maggie arrives, give her good directions to Lost River and tell her to step on it."

"And then you boot his English bum out of the house?"

I nodded. "And the rest of him too."

I got up. "I'm going to call the garage about a new back window."

Chapter 4

St. Jude's Catholic Church sat in the center of a half-acre lot. On the right side of the building, a royal poinciana tree sheltered a glass case filled with candles and a picture of Jesus. On the left side, two green painted picnic tables flanked a plaster statue of St. Francis of Assisi and a bird bath. There were only two ways to enter the church: a side door that faced the picnic tables and the big double doors in front of the building.

At a little past six that evening, I trailed Stubb Flanders past the poinciana tree to the rear of the church. It was half an hour after sunset, and I was loaded down with a tripod, camera bags, lawn chairs, a folding stool and coffee thermoses. I felt like a native bearer, real heart-of-darkness stuff.

Stubb, comfortable in his role of great white hunter, strode back and forth behind the church, sussing out the perfect place to sit. He was still upset about his missing gun and had bitched about it most of the twelve-mile drive to Lost River. I'd let the complaints flow over my head and right out my shattered back window.

Just as we reached the outskirts of town, he directed me down a street that was mostly dirt road and said he had to pick up his clothes. While I waited out front, engine running, he let himself into a cement block house and returned five minutes later, carrying a backpack. It was obvious to me that he'd had a drink or two while inside; he was much cheerier when he got back in the car. So cheery, in fact, that he shared his plan for the evening. Which was interesting, because it didn't just involve my help, it tied me up until Maggie arrived to relieve me.

Stubb eventually picked the back corner of the church as a stake-out site, and I set up his lawn chair with the coffee thermoses beside it. Fortunately for him, the church had sprung for street lights when St. Jude's became a thriving tourist destination. Most of them were located out front, but one had been placed in the back near a stand of trees. From his chair, Stubb could see the entire back section of the church, as well as anyone approaching the side door near the picnic tables. Watching the side door was critical. It was the only other entrance to the building.

Stubb stood behind the folding chair, hands on hips, eyes moving along the back wall of the church. He really was a good-looking guy. Even his premature wrinkling seemed sophisticated rather than degenerate. He was muttering to himself. ". . . shadow fill . . . contrast . . . gradated filter . . ."

I felt a momentary liking for him. Photography was one thing Stubb and I agreed on; shooting pictures the old tried-and-true way, with ASA 400 Tri X fast black and white. It gave you tonal quality and grain and texture, instead of that shiny, ultra-smooth digital look.

"All right, then." He turned to face me, dead serious. "I watch the back of the church and the side door; you cover the front entrance. Nobody gets in the place without one of us seeing them. Do not move, even an inch. Stay in place until I come get you."

I stifled a laugh. He sounded like a line from my favorite movie, *The Longest Day*: "Hold until relieved. Hold until relieved." I nearly saluted. Instead, I said, "What about all the windows?"

"The stained glass ones on either side of the church don't matter. They only open a few inches at the bottom, and besides, they're wired."

"No, I meant that one." I pointed at the only window in the back wall, a frosty-paned, fourteen-inch square about six feet off the ground.

"Unimportant. That's in the room next to the dirt room." Stubb adjusted the Bluetooth stuck in his ear and flopped into the lawn chair. "I can do without supervising. Get around front."

He was so arrogant, I debated driving home and leaving piglet boy to whoever wanted to beat him up next. But by the time I trekked around to the front entrance — through the yard on the north side this time — I was over it. I was doing this for Maggie, not Stubb. Maggie had gone to bat for me when it really counted.

On the way, I stopped at the bird bath, reached for my camera and snapped Stubb leaning back in his chair, coffee in hand, feet propped on the stool, listening to whatever was on his iPod. From this distance, he looked totally blissed out. Obviously, he preferred his own company.

I put my own lawn chair on the sidewalk facing the main entrance and took several shots of the double doors, which were heavy, wooden and carved by somebody who knew how. The camera still felt odd in my hands, which was no surprise; I hadn't used one in nearly three years, not since the day my ex-husband smashed himself to bits driving drunk. But, in June, a friend had gifted me with a Nikon D90, a 70-30 telephoto lens, two SD chips and the suggestion that I move on, if not forward. There would never be a day I didn't prefer film, but as Kenji, one of my tenants and a professional photographer himself, kept reminding me, it was absolutely a digital world.

The evening was cool/pleasant verging on cool/chilly, and I was glad I'd worn a hoodie over my blue jeans and T-shirt. In the winter, inland Florida gets five to ten degrees cooler at night than coastal Florida. If you forget that, you'll be sorry.

I'd just found a comfortable position in the lawn chair when a priest appeared on the front steps, closed the double doors and locked them behind him. I recognized him because the local papers had run his picture every day during the initial miracle business and several times since. Father Mike Durkin, looking as Irish as his last name, was still at St. Jude's, having survived the miracle earth hoopla.

I looked at my watch, twenty-nine minutes past six. I got a dozen good shots of him, cassock swirling around his ankles, face somber. His brooding look was perfect. He could have been strolling the grounds at the Vatican, planning the next raid on the annoying Saracens.

He started down the sidewalk, then stopped and detoured over to where I sat. I got quickly to my feet, as if I'd done something wrong. "Hello, Father."

"Good evening." He looked from my camera to my chair.

"Is it your colleague, then, who's sitting behind the church?"

I nodded, embarrassed to admit it I knew a guy who went berserk when not allowed to photograph magic dirt. Father Mike merely nodded and continued on his way. His shoulders slumped a little as he walked, a man of God with too much on his mind, it seemed. A few seconds later, I snapped that too.

After that, nothing happened at all, unless you counted the people who wandered by and stared at me sitting in front of the church, then walked around back to see Stubb doing the same thing and apparently went home to tell their families and friends about it. It was growing colder, and I checked my watch again. Maggie must be en route; another hour or so and I could head home.

Around nine p.m., three guys in long-sleeved shirts and jeans ambled into the churchyard and flopped down on one of the picnic tables. They were carrying six packs of Coke, but there was obviously something besides soda in those tinny little cans. Their voices got steadily louder as they spiked their *cola* from the contents of a paper bag, and their laughter had an edge to it. All three were facing the side door that led to the earth room.

After glancing in their direction several times, I decided it was the same three guys from the Whole Hog Saloon in about the same state of inebriation as the night before. I took a quick picture when they weren't looking my way then watched to make sure they didn't go around back and pound hell out of Maggie's intended. From that angle, they had a clear view of Stubb sprawled in his lawn chair.

At nine thirty-five, two backpackers and a blonde woman pulling a canvas suitcase arrived to share the front sidewalk with me. The backpackers, a twenty-something couple, were on a mission. They'd hiked all the way from Cedar Key and intended to be the first people through the front door next morning. The guy, Eddie, with a last name I missed, was tall with long dark hair and a beard. His companion, Cara, looked a lot like him, minus the facial hair. The woman with the suitcase, who introduced herself as Lee Lee, had come up on the bus from Miami and was so excited about getting a glimpse of the magic dirt, she was almost incoherent.

Lee Lee's white-blonde hair was swept to the left side of her head in a thick braid, and she was either twenty-eight or forty-eight; her skin was so smooth, it was hard to tell. She was into music, or at least into making songs from the last word anyone else uttered. When the Cedar Key couple began a sentence with "People say," Lee Lee broke into song and segued into Smokey Robinson's "The Tracks of My Tears," which pretty much put a stop to that conversation.

When she heard somebody was watching the church around back, Lee Lee dumped her suitcase and pranced around past the picnic tables to check Stubb out. She returned a couple of minutes later with a bewildered look.

"He told me to get lost," she said in a little girl voice. "He's not very nice, huh?"

I said no, not very, and hid my surprise. It wasn't the old Stubb's style to run off a hot-looking blonde. Or any blonde, as long as she had the requisite parts.

At twenty past ten, a much older woman arrived in a maroon Range Rover with a roll bar. She parked on a nearby side street, jumped out and strode in our direction, energy radiating out of her heeled cowboy boots.

"Hi!" she called out to me as she got closer. "Candy Butler. I got this phone call a little bit ago — said there was a problem down here. What's going on?"

I eyed her. I was pretty sure we'd never met, and I didn't recognize the name. She had dark eyes, curly-black, chemically treated hair, and she wasn't overweight, just big boned and wiry. Wrestling a recalcitrant steer was probably no big deal to her. I stood up as she approached because I'm not okay with being cornered in a flimsy lawn chair, and she looked like somebody who'd do that.

"I said," she repeated, "what's going on?"

I grinned at her. "A friend wanted to come to St. Jude's, and I drove him out here."

"A friend called Flanders?" Her black eyes flashed for a second. "Where is the famous photographer, then? Can't be inside. Not all locked up with the alarm set and everything."

Lee Lee from Miami spoke up. "If you mean the guy with the cameras, he's sitting behind the church."

The black eyes flashed at her too. "Doing what?"

"I'm not sure," the girl admitted. "I went to say hi, but he told me to scram."

"Where is he, exactly?"

"Around the back corner to the left, but I don't think I'd bother him . . ."

"Honey, I'm not going to bother the boy. I'm going to tear him a new one." Candy Butler swung around and headed in the opposite direction from the one Lee Lee had indicated. "I'll go this way, come up on his blind side."

"Who is *she*?" Lee Lee said in a voice of awe.

I lifted my camera and got several shots of an aggravated woman rounding the corner of the church, arms swinging, walking toe-first like John Wayne.

"Not sure," I said, "but I think she might be the rancher who put out an expensive brochure about St. Jude's dirt. I heard the story at the grocery store yesterday, and if that's her, Stubb got on her wrong side the second day he hit town."

Lee Lee murmured a few bars from "My Kind of Town."

I moved the camera in her direction. "You mind if I take your picture?"

"No, but what for? Are you a photographer, too?"

"Not really, just reviving an old habit I thought I'd given up." And, I admitted to myself, taking a few shots that Maggie might be glad to have, if Stubb kept to his current level of endeavor. For two weeks, he'd apparently done nothing but measure the levels in the earth room. You don't make an entire magazine article out of dirt. No matter who you are.

I snapped several pictures of Lee Lee and the couple from Cedar Key, noting how little illumination the street lights actually provided. In the old days, shooting in the dark didn't just feel different, it was different, and you had to work at it. This new camera had a built-in flash that obliterated the need for remote shutter releases and adjustable light meters. It sounded good, but I wouldn't be sure until Kenji, my self-appointed technical advisor, had a look at my downloaded shots. I clicked off a few more shots of the three guys in the side yard, who were now sprawled on top of the picnic table.

It was probably fifteen minutes before Candy Butler came back, and she wasn't smiling.

"Well, I waited around, but he musta heard me coming and went off to hide in the bushes."

"He's not there?" I said, frowning.

"Oh, he's there, all right. The coffee in his cup is still hot, and his stuff's piled around his camp chair. He's either taking a leak or waiting for me to leave." She looked at her watch.

"I'll give him enough time to feel safe, then I'll go back and straighten that boy out."

She dropped down into a sitting position on the grass between my chair and Lee Lee's sleeping bag and let out a deep sigh. "Wish I had a cup of coffee. Should've taken his, but I was afraid I'd catch something."

Lee Lee brightened immediately, foraged in her back pack and pulled out a thermos. "It's already got cream and sugar," she offered tentatively.

"Just the way I like it." Candy Butler accepted a brown, recycled-paper cup, took a healthy sip and made a visible effort to be friendly.

Lee Lee segued into the refrain from "That's the Way I Like It," à la K.C. and the Sunshine Band.

Ms. Butler was actually very pleasant when she put her mind to it and smiled, which she did frequently during the next hour. You could see she'd probably been a knockout at twenty. She started out talking cattle and horses and the old days in Florida. Then she found out Lee Lee had graduated from an Arizona astrology school, and they had a spirited discussion about actual healing versus psychosomatic healing, spiritual vortexes and titanium body wraps. Then, in an obvious effort to include me, she insisted on knowing the story of what I did: part-time instructor at the college, where I lived: a house in Seminole Beach, and who I lived with: a writer, an ikebana expert, a weaver, a potter and a cook.

Lee Lee chipped in at that point with how she'd love to live in a place with all that creativity, and Ms. Butler, who also seemed fascinated with the idea of a houseful of artists, wanted to know what had made me think of it.

"Not my idea," I admitted. "My friend Amy wanted a quiet

place to write a cookbook, and I rented her a room. Then she decided the place was too quiet and talked me into renting the rest of the rooms to a bunch of art-grant recipients. She did all the work, even put elegant, spelled-out numbers on the bedroom doors and collected the rents."

"You seem like a normal person," Candy Butler said, then gestured toward the rear of the church. "Why are you helping that jerk do a job on St. Jude's?"

"I'm not," I assured her. "Stubb was supposed to write an article about the healing room, but he made a name for himself years ago exposing scams and I think he decided to go for it again. He's really hung up on the amount of dirt available every day."

"Oh, God, that awful brochure." Ms. Butler rubbed her forehead with the fingers of her left hand until she made red splotches.

"I beg your pardon?"

Her head jerked back and forth. "When we first found out about the earth — when the boy, Andreas, suddenly spoke after playing in it — and people started telling how they'd been healed, I got a brainstorm. Father Mike was against it, but I thought it would be good for the town. So I wrote a brochure and paid to have it printed and distributed — a couple thousand copies. I wrote that there was plenty of earth, and you could take away as much as you wanted because there was always enough left for the next person who needed a miracle."

She made a sound in her throat and looked away. "Then Father Mike said it sounded like the dirt itself was magic and was replacing itself, so I changed that line and rounded up as many of the old copies as possible. But that . . . Flanders got hold of some of them. He's trying to make us all look like a bunch of liars. He was completely impossible when he came out to the ranch." She looked up at me. "But he's your friend; you must know what he's like."

"We were acquaintances more than friends, and I haven't seen him in years," I told her. "But somebody who is a close friend asked me to . . . help him out. She's flying in tonight. Maybe she can get him to see reason."

Ms. Butler didn't look like she believed that any more than I did. She checked the time again. "Okay, eleven-thirty. Let's see if he's still hiding." She stood up and headed around the church again, this time more quietly.

I snapped another shot to show the contrast.

She returned almost immediately. "Either that boy's just plain lucky or he's taken off somewhere."

"It's possible," I said. "He has a thing for Lost River's bars."

She pulled a face. "I heard something about that. He oughta be careful. People around here don't like him much." She stood around for a couple of minutes longer before giving up. "Well, ladies, it was fun, but I've wasted enough time on Mr. Flanders, and I got a bed calling me. Thanks for the coffee and conversation."

I took a few more pictures as she walked to the Range Rover, started it up and backed out onto the main road. It was very quiet after she roared down the highway. I looked at my watch again. Where the hell could Stubb be at almost midnight? For that matter, where was Maggie? I pulled out my cell phone and called Amy, who was still awake but hadn't heard anything. Then I punched in Maggie's number.

Chapter 5

Maggie's phone rang six times before she answered, and she sounded groggy with sleep. "Sorry, Keegan . . . missed . . . the plane . . . early flight out of LaGuardia. I'll be there . . . by noon." She hung up before I had a chance to tell her where Stubb and I were.

I tapped in Amy's phone number.

"What's the matter?" Lee Lee had been openly listening to my phone conversation.

"Oh, nothing. I may be here all night, after all."

"Good." Lee Lee hummed a stanza of "All Night Long," then offered, "I'll have somebody to talk to. Don't forget, I brought plenty of food in case you get hungry."

When Amy answered, she suggested I leave Stubb where he was and come home, but I figured as soon as his coffee ran out, he'd call it a night. I told her I'd hang on for another hour.

Around midnight, the temperature took a dive. It does that in December. You go to bed at a perfectly respectable seventy-two degrees and wake up with a high of forty-five. I zipped up the hoodie, but it didn't do much good.

The people who'd been walking up and down the street disappeared to their nice warm houses. A group of eight Boy Scouts arrived at one o'clock with snacks and iPhones. They zipped themselves into sleeping bags and immediately started texting each other. The three guys at the picnic table packed up their empty Coke cans and went off on foot. I got a great picture of them shivering in their thin shirts. Only one had a jacket, and he had it pulled clear up around his ears. Apparently, they gave a rats about Stubb's stake-out; they just wanted a comfortable place to get snockered.

Lee Lee took her backpack and went to the Porta-Potty across the street before all the Boy Scouts decided they had to relieve themselves at once. When she returned, wrapped in a heavy cotton sweater, I visited it myself. Unfortunately, I had no heavy sweater, and by one-thirty in the morning I was frozen, beyond bored and starving to death. I was seriously considering Lee Lee's quinoa-and-lentil concoction — which I'd refused twice already — when a vehicle roared by, braked, reversed and stopped in front of the church. It was a greenish-yellow Jeep that looked like it had rolled down a hill at least twice. Amy was behind the wheel, and Bear and Kenji were squeezed in around a couple of giant wicker baskets. They were all wearing coats.

"What're you guys doing out in the middle of the night?" I said, hoping the baskets Bear was pulling out of the back seat meant food. Kenji unloaded folding chairs, blankets and an iPad, and Amy drove away to park.

"Amy thought you might need a little sustenance since your friend Maggie crapped out on you," Bear said. "Kenji's along because he's sensitive. He can't sleep when the temperature drops twenty degrees."

When Amy came back, I introduced them all to Lee Lee, who ditched her lentils and demolished a roast beef sandwich just as if she wasn't a practicing vegetarian. I ate two ham and provolone myself and poured café mocha from one of the thermoses. The smell of rich, milky coffee laced with chocolate liqueur filled the frigid air.

"So," Lee Lee took in Bear's dark hair, blue eyes and wide shoulders, her own eyes filled with speculation. "Keegan said she's got a house full of artists. What kind are you?"

Amy eyed Lee Lee over her brown, recycled-paper cup with a half smile. She's used to women moving in on Bear.

I wrapped myself in one of the blankets and intervened before Bear ventured into lengthy explanation. "Bear's a writer, and Kenji's an ikebana expert who does underwater digital photography. Amy, as you probably noticed, is the best cook around. She published a cookbook last year and is working on another one."

Lee Lee eyed Amy, appraised Bear a second time then shifted her attention to Kenji. "Aren't there five of you at Keegan's house?"

Kenji gazed back at her solemnly and twisted his thick, wiry hair into a ponytail with one hand. "Yes. Five. But Jesse was . . . too tired to get up, and Nita catches plane to Chicago today."

"What kind of art do they do?"

"Nita embroiders giant screens of Florida history — very beautiful. And Jesse is a potter who . . . sculpts. Also very good."

"Where's your buddy, Stubb?" Amy said. "He just leave you here to do all the work?"

I stretched luxuriously under my warm blanket. "Staking out the back of the church, I think. A woman went around to see him a little while ago, but he wasn't in his chair. He may be hiding. She wasn't a fan."

"You didn't go yourself?"

"I did not. He told me to stay here with my eyes on the front door of the church until he came to get me, and I don't care if he freezes his ass off. I don't want him telling Maggie somebody slipped in a boat load of miracle earth when I was distracted. He's probably been holed up in some bar for hours, but I'm not moving from this spot until he comes to relieve me or the priest shows up."

"That's at six forty-five," Lee Lee put in, flipping her braid around. "I can't wait to get inside. Have any of you seen the magic earth? Does it look really different than regular earth?"

I was the only one in the house who'd been to the earth room, but that was years ago and it hadn't made much of an impression on me, even then.

"It's just dirt," I told her. "Not the stuff they call muck, like around Lake Okeechobee. And not the sandy kind around here that's good for citrus. It's like something off the bottom of the river, if you dried it out. It looked slightly greenish, but that could just have been the lack of light. There was only a single bulb on in the room when I saw it."

Lee Lee nodded, her face thoughtful. "Somebody who got healed there said the atmosphere was so intense you could feel it the second you walked through the door. They said the air was heavy with the most amazing sense of hope."

"Heavy with something, I expect, especially in summer with minimal air conditioning and no window."

Lee Lee smiled at me serenely and sang something about a doggie in a window.

The next two hours passed faster than I expected, as the temperature continued to inch down. Lee Lee talked to Amy about rolfing, whatever that was; I took more pictures, what I would have called several rolls in the old days; Bear went to sleep in his chair; and Kenji was on his iPad, looking up the history of Lost River.

Kenji has changed more than anybody in the house. His razor-cut hair, pressed khakis and polished loafers morphed to Birkenstocks, cargo shorts and a Diana Ross frizz mere months after he moved in. "American girls do not like neat men," he once informed me with great seriousness. He's also quiet, shy and self-effacing until he finds some new piece of information he assumes you're dying to hear.

He began relating Lost River's origins, starting with a shipwrecked Spanish priest who trekked inland to a dried-up river bed and built a mission. Actually, his faithful Indian helpers built the place while the good father supervised. They named it Rio Perdido, AKA Lost River, but fever eventually wiped out the helpers, and the Florida climate ate away the wood and clay buildings. There was also something about Seminole Indians, but I was dozing by then and missed it.

Around four, Amy began to pack up. "Sure you don't want to come home with us?" she said, nudging me. "You don't owe Stubb anything. Sitting around here is a waste of time."

I looked at my watch. "I've already wasted most of the night. Besides, I promised Maggie. I will, however, keep an extra blanket."

Amy handed me two, and Kenji took my camera chip. "Will

download these at home, check what you have done," he promised.

The last two hours dragged. I couldn't sleep sitting in the chair, but when I got up and walked around, the temperature forced me back under the blankets. By six forty, I was stiff with cold and inactivity. The campers began to get to their feet and assemble their belongings, but there was no sign of Stubb. He was probably tucked away in some local woman's nice, cozy bed, some local woman who was a sucker for an English accent and didn't mind popping for a bar tab. Or maybe he'd returned to the house where we'd picked up his gear.

I stomped my feet for warmth and clicked off a string of pictures: Lee Lee, the Cedar Key couple, the Boy Scouts, Father Mike as he came down the sidewalk at six forty-four, climbed the steps of the church and unlocked the front doors.

Old Stubb had either overslept or was hung over; otherwise, he'd have met the priest at the door and dogged him down the aisle. Maybe even patted him down to make sure he wasn't hiding a bagful of dirt under his black robes.

Father Mike reappeared suddenly in the open front doors. He looked around the waiting group of people, fixed his gaze on me and came down the steps. He took my arm and led me aside.

"It's your photographer friend," he said quietly. "He's lying in the back room, and I think he's been dead for some time."

Chapter 6

Priest or not, I didn't believe him. He might just as well have said I'd won the lottery. A host of scenarios flashed into my mind: Stubb had managed somehow to get in the church and was playing a gigantic hoax on all of us; Father Mike, for reasons known only to him, was playing a gigantic hoax on me; somebody who looked like Stubb was dead in the dirt room, and Father Mike needed glasses; nobody was dead in the dirt room, and Father Mike needed a shrink.

"You're going to have to show me," I managed to squeak out. "He's playing some kind of trick . . ."

Father Mike patted my arm. "I have to call the police. Let's find a place for you to sit . . ."

"No." I shook him off. "If this really happened, you'll have to show me."

The priest's face settled into lines of disapproval, but after a quick look at the group out front, he escorted me back into the church, shut and locked the doors behind us and led the way down the main aisle to the vestry.

It was slightly warmer inside than out, but ominously silent, like the building was holding its breath. Or maybe it was just me. The painted colors of the wooden altar, silvery greens and reds and golds, jumped out at me as we turned left at a roughly carved Christ on an elongated wood cross. We passed through a little, rounded doorway leading into the back hall. A further arched door led to the famous, empty, whitewashed room.

Only the room was no longer empty. In its center, Stubb Flanders, still clutching a camera, lay half-in, half-out of a large circle of healing earth. There was blood on his trademark chambray shirt and also on his tripod, which had fallen — or been thrown — a few feet away.

I made a noise that was part protest, part pain. For a couple of seconds, I wasn't in St. Jude's at all; I was back on my uncle's farm in Ohio, squatting beside a pink and white baby pig with a black band around its middle. The pig's eyes were open, and it didn't move, but in my seven-year-old mind, I was sure all it needed was a blanket and a little tender loving care. I was patting its side when my uncle appeared.

"It's dead, Keegan, leave it alone."

When I insisted I could feel it breathing, he shook his head. "It's too stiff. It's gone."

Stubb was gone too. He was too stiff, too sprawled, too clearly not there anymore.

The pig had been tossed in a ditch later, and I couldn't shake that picture from my mind. I also couldn't move out of the doorway. Maybe I'd be stuck here forever, staring at a dead man who'd been beaten to death with his own camera tripod, a man I had never really known. I squeezed my eyes until Stubb's body blurred behind a thick screen of eyelashes.

"Please come away." Father Mike's quiet voice echoed in the small room. "There's nothing that can be done, and I have to call the police. I've already delayed too long."

I opened my eyes, shoved a shaking hand in my pocket and offered him my cell phone. When he looked blankly at me, I punched in 911 and put it in his hand.

I watched him as he spoke, more to keep from staring at Stubb than anything else. Father Mike didn't look like a priest today, in spite of his long-skirted, black cassock. He just looked like the Irishman he was, middle height, thick-set, reddish hair, cut short with some gray on the sides. Smile lines in a face that was not smiling now.

I shivered in the cold room. There was an odd smell here, something beyond the odor of damp and whitewash and cement, a smell that didn't belong. I sniffed twice more before I identified it: the fresh, clean scent of earth and grass after it rains.

A sheriff's deputy was the first to arrive at the church. He told us he was securing the scene and to stay where we were until the detectives arrived. That wasn't good news for people who'd been waiting outside all night. The Boy Scout leader was still in mid-protest when the sheriff's cars began rolling in.

In the three or so hours it took to get a search warrant and find a judge to sign it, the deputies didn't dally. Crime scene tape went up immediately around the building and grounds, and we were all moved from the sidewalk to a grassy area beside the church yard. The press, who had begun to gather like buzzards smelling a good thing, congregated across the road near the Porta-Potty units. Some stood in the middle of the road, shooting pictures and blocking traffic.

Everyone who'd been in front of the church was interviewed separately, starting with the Boy Scouts, who gave enthusiastic, recorded, verbal statements. When the detectives read everyone their Miranda rights, "just to be on the safe side," the scouts achieved near ecstasy and were openly disappointed when told they could leave.

The couple from Cedar Key, Lee Lee and I were less enthralled.

The detective, who gave his name as Christensen, spent quite a lot of time with me, taking notes and also recording me. I explained who Stubb was and that his plan was to actually catch somebody bringing magic dirt into the earth room. What I couldn't explain was how he had entered a locked building without tripping the alarm, although I thought I knew why.

"Father Mike refused to let cameras inside," I told Christensen. "Stubb always had a reputation for getting the story he wanted, no matter who told him no."

"But you didn't go around to check on him all night?" The detective persisted. "And he didn't come around to check in with you?"

I explained that Stubb had ordered me to stay put, and I did, and was waiting for him to give me the word. I don't think he found my account particularly compelling, but he didn't get difficult about it. I also told him about Ms. Butler's visit and my friends bringing food and blankets in the early morning hours.

He asked me to stick around for awhile and went to talk to Lee Lee.

Sometime before noon, crime scene personnel arrived, and St. Jude's began to resemble the set of a reality crime show. Officers in protective suits went in and out of the church, transferring brown evidence bags and other items to their truck. Other officers videoed inside the church then moved outside to record the two side yards, the back and even the underbrush adjoining the property. Overhead, a police helicopter took aerial pictures.

In lieu of eyewitness reports, the press, who were still languishing across the street, did their best with zoom lenses and the occasional interview of a local. Several dozen people had gathered as close to the scene as possible, and drivers kept slowing down and had to be encouraged on their way.

Eventually, Stubb's body was removed.

After all the commotion, it was anticlimatic when Lee Lee, the Cedar Key couple, Father Mike and I were invited to the sheriff's department for further discussion.

The substation was a long, low, cream painted building. It had a red-orange tiled roof that gave it an adobe look and stone-colored tile floors. Inside was a big, bulletproof window, disguised as a mirror, so you ended up talking to a reflection of your own face while waiting for a disembodied voice behind the glass to respond. It was unnerving, but it beat being brought through the back in a prisoner van.

As we entered the front door, Candy Butler was just coming out. She was wearing jeans, boots, a leather jacket and a scowl. Her eyes slid past me without recognition as she tromped out the door.

Father Mike was interviewed first, at his request, then departed to prepare a special mass for those who were missing the regularly scheduled one.

By the time Detective Christensen got around to me, I was halfway through a third cup of the hot, black coffee provided by the dispatcher and no longer shaky inside and out. But I couldn't get my head around the fact that Stubb just — wasn't — anymore. I kept thinking that if he'd flown back to New York or London, or Calcutta even, he'd have been just as out of sight, just as gone. None of it seemed real. Yesterday I'd driven to the Whole Hog to pick him up, today he didn't exist.

Christensen was pleasant, but he read me the Miranda warning again, which unnerved me further.

I was glad I hadn't done anything wrong then wondered if he was as sure about that as I was.

His questions were repeats of the ones I'd already answered, with variations: when had I first met Stubb Flanders; how well did I know him; what, precisely, was our relationship.

I repeated that I hadn't seen Stubb for a dozen years or better, that an old friend had asked me to check on him while he was in Florida and that he'd spent the night at my house.

Christensen asked for the name of the New York friend, and I gave it to him, but I didn't tell him she was on her way to Florida. This was going to be a god-awful mess, and the last thing Maggie needed was to be mixed up in Stubb's murder.

The detective finished making notes then settled back in his chair.

"It's hard to believe Mr. Flanders didn't come around to check with you the entire night. Or that you didn't go around back to check on him. That you didn't communicate for," he glanced over at his notebook, "nearly twelve hours?"

When I didn't have a new answer for that question, he asked me to do a time line for the last twenty-four hours. That wasn't difficult; I'd done little more than eyeball my watch during most of the time he was interested in. I talked, and he keyed in my responses.

When we finished, he studied his laptop. "Your friend, Luanne Keiner, says she was talking to you all night and neither one of you moved from around ten o'clock on, except to visit the Porta-Potty across the road. And, to use her own words, 'something should be done about those things. They're disgusting, the flies and the smell! What if somebody pushed you over and the door side was down, and you were stuck in there and couldn't get out . . .' "

I grinned, in spite of myself. "That sounds like Lee Lee. Her name's really Luane?"

"You didn't know that?"

I shook my head. "Never saw her before last night, when she showed up with the couple from Cedar Key."

"Oh, yeah, Eddie and Cara Ortega."

Christensen printed out a copy of the time line and slid it across the desk to me.

"Let's look at it again, one item at a time. See how it shakes out."

I nodded, studying my own words through tired eyes.

Wednesday, PM

8:00 — Drove to Lost River. Met Stubb Flanders at the Whole Hog, brought him back to spend the night in Seminole Beach.

Thursday, PM

5:55 — Drove Stubb from Seminole Beach to Lost River, stopped at the edge of town to pick up his backpack, and settled him behind the church.

6:29 — Father Mike locked church doors and left.
9:00 — Three men came to sit on picnic bench in St Jude's side yard and drink.
9:30 — Lee Lee arrived with couple from Cedar Key, went around to see Stubb and got shooed away.
10:20 — Candy Butler arrived, went to back of church to find Stubb.
10:35 — Ms. Butler returned to front of church and sat, talking.
11:30 — Ms. Butler went to back of church again, returned, drove away.

Friday, AM

1:00 — Boy scouts arrived. Three men on picnic bench woke up and left.
1:30 — Amy, Kenji and Bear arrived with food and blankets.
4:00 — Amy, Kenji and Bear left.
6:45 — Father Mike unlocked church doors.
6:50 — Father Mike returned to say he'd found Stubb's body.

I looked up at him and nodded. "Pretty close. Maybe off five minutes or so."

"Those three guys at the picnic table. You're sure they didn't go near the church? Didn't walk around? Go to the john? Anything like that?"

"Not while I was watching. They were probably the same three I saw the night before at a place called the Whole Hog Saloon. Stubb was there too, making himself obnoxious to everybody, and when they turned up at St. Jude's,

I thought they might be there to cause trouble. But they just drank and slept."

"You're sure they left at one? Ms. Keiner thought it was later, maybe two thirty."

I shook my head. "My friends brought food at one thirty. It was before that."

"Okay."

Christensen asked for a description of the three men, and I did my best, but thinnish, brown guys in white shirts and blue jeans tend to look alike. Never mind their tendency to sprawl face-down on furniture.

When he asked about the pictures I'd taken during the evening, I handed over my camera and got a nasty surprise: He kept it. In exchange, I got a piece of paper promising it would be returned to me when it was no longer needed for evidence.

Then he took me through my story again.

By the time I left the substation, I was like the walking dead who don't know they're dead. I sidestepped two errant members of the press who were camped outside and made it to my car, unmolested. Then I called Amy, who was sound asleep. She couldn't believe Stubb was dead at all, let alone murdered.

"God, that's awful," she muttered. "Who did it?"

"Nobody knows. They don't even know how he got in the church."

"What do I say to Maggie when she shows up?"

"I don't know. Nothing, I guess. Keep her there. I'll be home in half an hour."

It was more like forty-five minutes, because Lee Lee waved me down as I drove past St. Jude's. She was practically standing in the street with her suitcase, looking confused and upset. When I pulled over, she hopped in and started to babble immediately.

Eddie and Cara Ortega from Cedar Key were taking a room at the Mikasuki Inn, she told me, more determined than ever to see the miracle earth. The Boy Scouts were gone. Lee Lee herself, disturbed by the kharmic implications of Stubb's death in a healing environment (her words), wanted to stick around another twenty-four hours until the yellow crime scene tape was removed from the dirt room. But if she did, she was going to have to camp out because she didn't have enough cash for a hotel room and bus fare, and did I think camping out on the street was against the law in Lost River?

Which is how I ended up with Lee Lee as a passenger as I drove back to Seminole Beach. If I'd had the energy, I'd have banged my head on the steering wheel. First Stubb, then Maggie, now Lee Lee AKA Luane Keiner. All because of a very old debt.

Lee Lee chattered nonstop all the way home, but most of her comments floated right past me. Except once, when the wind was blowing her hair around and we were both shivering and she said in a thoughtful voice, "Did you ever think of getting a back window for this car?"

Everyone who sees my house for the first time is surprised, and Lee Lee was no exception. Even in Seminole Beach, where no house matched its neighbor in style or conception, 32 East River was an oddity — big, barny New England surrounded by cinder block and stucco-on-termite contemporaries. It had been built in the fifties by a Rhode Island transplant whose idea of paradise was three stories of clapboard siding with a water view.

"Wow!" Lee Lee got out of the car, eyes wide. "*This* is your place? All of it?"

I nodded. I'm not house-proud in any way, but it is a classy-looking place: white clapboard with black shutters, bay windows and a widow's walk at the top. Colonial revival, I think they call it.

"I got it in the divorce. One of my ex's notorious trades. It was the only thing he owned free and clear."

"Wow. You must have been so excited to move in."

"Not really."

I didn't tell her I'd been living at the beach in a cottage I dubbed "womb with a view," while trying to recover from the double whammy of failing at marriage and losing Jack in a car crash before I'd had time to get over him. Or that I wouldn't have moved into the house at all if I hadn't been flooded out of the cottage.

The smell of something cooking in butter and cream and wine drifted through the back door as Lee Lee and I entered. The kitchen was warm, and Amy was stirring something in a huge kettle. She looked up and reported, "Still no sign of Maggie."

"Probably just as well. I'm not looking forward to breaking the news about Stubb." I tossed down the blankets I'd brought in from the car. "This is Lee Lee. I told her she could stay here a couple of days until St. Jude's earth room reopens."

"Sure." Amy grinned at her. "You can have Room Number Two, next to Nita. If Maggie ever shows up, she can go in Number Three, next to where Stubb stayed — if it doesn't creep her out."

I got sheets and towels out of the closet, showed Lee Lee the second floor bathroom, reminded her it was shared and left her to make up the bed in Number Two.

Then I went downstairs and talked Amy out of a bowl of the corn and scallop chowder she was making. I had just swallowed a hot, buttery mouthful when the front door opened and slammed shut. Footsteps sounded in the hallway as I looked up to see who was making all the racket.

Maggie Gilchrist stumbled into the kitchen without knocking or calling out to see if anybody was home. She was in tears, but after a few seconds of myopic squinting, she seemed to recognize me and threw both arms around my neck, sobbing.

"Stubb. Oh, Stubb, oh, God, Stubb. It's all my fault."

As I said, I hadn't seen Maggie in years, but the woman strangling me was nothing like the one I'd worked with in London. Maggie was English, for God's sake; she hadn't even cried at her mother's funeral. I stood there, awkward and uncomfortable, patting at her shoulder. She was thin, much thinner than I remembered.

Eventually, Amy pulled Maggie off me, sat her in a kitchen chair and applied an ice bag to her neck. Then she told me to boil some water in a hurry.

When I looked confused, she rolled her dark eyes in disgust and said, "For tea, Keegan. The English use it like a tranquilizer, right? A cure for everything?"

I boiled the water, pulled a teapot off the shelf and shoveled loose tea into it.

"On . . . the . . . radio . . ." Maggie finally got out between sobs. "My fault. I got him this job, made him take it . . . I'm so . . ." And she went off into spasms again.

When the tea had steeped, Amy poured out a cup and diluted it with milk. "Get some of this down her, if you can. I'll make up the bed in Number Three."

I coaxed some tea down Maggie, holding the cup because her shaking hands weren't going to do anything but dump it over both of us, and waited for Amy to come back. When she did, we helped my old friend up to the second floor and into bed. Amy gave her a glass of water and a couple of aspirins, and watched while she took them.

I could almost hear the house filling up again. This place seemed to abhor a vacuum. I glanced into Lee Lee's room as we came back out on the landing. Her door was wide open, and she was sacked out, fully clothed, on top of the unmade bed.

"Where's Bear?" I whispered to Amy.

"Still asleep. Kenji too. I haven't seen Jesse. He's such a hermit these days, he could be dead in his room, for all I know."

"Okay, then. I guess I'll go see if Maggie's got luggage in her car. If she actually came here in a car. After that, I'm going to crash too."

"You're . . ." Amy began, then stopped and cocked her head. "Is that the doorbell? I didn't know it worked."

"Somebody must have fixed it. I'll see who's here."

Two plain-clothes deputies stood on the front porch. One held up his identification.

"Afternoon, ma'am, we'd like to speak to Amy Casella, Zack Day and Kenji Shu. I understand they were at St. Jude's church in Lost River early this morning."

I motioned them into the hall and managed not to groan out loud.

Nobody has ever called Bear Zack, just like nobody knows where in the west he really comes from. Idaho, I think. Someplace remote, anyway. I left the officers with Amy and went upstairs. Maggie and Lee Lee were dead to the world. I closed both their doors and went up to the third floor to wake Kenji and Bear.

One of the deputies did the interviews while the other eyeballed the kitchen and walked around, looking at the rest of the house. Eventually, he asked if he could see the room that Stubb had slept in, so I took him up to Number Four, opened the door and left him to it.

I waited in the hall until he came out, and when he asked to see *my* living space, led him down half a flight to the mezzanine, where he checked the bathroom, the towels and dirty clothes hamper, and each of my tiny rooms. As we exited into the main hallway, he asked if anyone else lived in the house. I didn't get into temporary guests who were currently sleeping and merely told him Jesse was on the sunporch.

Jesse's door was closed, and it was some time before he opened it and peered out at us. As Amy said, Jesse had been avoiding everybody since his fling with a young girl who had a problem with drugs and sharp knives. Today, he was mixing red clay on his potter's wheel, but he took time out to confirm that he had not accompanied the others to Lost River the night before and had never been to St. Jude's Church.

When we returned to the kitchen, the other deputy had finished with Kenji and Bear, who were nowhere in sight. He was now concentrating on Amy, who dislikes the police. Something to do with a cousin in New Jersey. The atmosphere was awkward, but the questions were repetitious rather than difficult: "What time did you arrive at the church?" "Did you sit there the whole night?" "What time did you leave?" "Did you drive straight home?"

Amy answered, but mostly with one word or less, an almost expressionless look on her face.

Twenty minutes later, they had thanked us and were gone.

I stumbled upstairs, pulled off my clothes and fell into bed, unwashed. I didn't have the energy to stand in a shower, even for ten seconds. Sometimes clean is just a guideline.

Chapter 7

Early the next morning, Kenji, who prefers his news via iPad, went out to round up the papers for the rest of us, and by nine a.m., the entire household, with the exception of Maggie Gilchrist, was in the kitchen soaking up pots of cappuccino along with small town scandal.

After fifteen years of obscurity, Stubb Flanders was once again a headliner. His death made the front page of the *Palm Beach Post*, the *Miami Herald*, the *Tampa Tribune* and an inside paragraph in the *New York Times*.

The *Seminole Beach Sentinel* had outdone itself. LOCKED ROOM MYSTERY marched across the front page in the same type they'd used for the Boston Marathon bombing. The reporter laid out the story of Stubb's demise like a detective story. Silent church, doors and windows locked for the night, burglar alarm set, penitent pilgrims — penitent? — waiting out front. Then the big finish: Catholic priest arrives for the early mass, turns off the alarm and finds Stubb Flanders, dead on a pile of magic earth.

There was even a drawing of the church, in case you were too thick to grasp the printed explanation. Little red arrows pointed out the locked windows on both sides of the church, green arrows indicated the locked front doors and the small side door.

There was an enlarged shot of the alarm keypad, located next to the side door, along with the name of the company that installed and monitored it. There was also a picture of the company representative, a twenty-something blonde in a very short skirt, who rushed to Lost River to inspect the system and spoke assertively to Channel 5.

"The alarm was not interfered with or disabled in any way. Anyone trying to break in, creep in or sneak in would have immediately triggered an ungodly — er — raucous blare that would continue until someone who knew the code could turn it off."

Since the alarm had not sounded, the *Sentinel* reporter posed two simple questions: "How did Stubb Flanders obtain entry to the earth room, and how did his killer get out?"

Amy, who dislikes the media nearly as much as the police, ignored the newspapers and plunged into a baking marathon that resulted in two kinds of bread pudding, one with bourbon sauce, and an enormous terrine of tiramisu.

Bear, of course, was all over the Locked Room Mystery. He'd already forgotten being one hundred percent wrong about the last case he "cracked" and kept reminding Kenji how the two of them had saved my "bacon" by rescuing me from a shotgun blast. Bear falls into clichés when he's keyed-up, which is probably why none of his books — the Hemingway knockoffs, the children's Bunny Adventures or his recent suspense novel — have yet to be published.

Lee Lee, like Maggie, had slept through the police visit and was unexpectedly subdued. It was possible she was just tired or that she'd talked enough the day before to get it all out of her system. Whichever, she studied the drawing of the church as if she was going to be tested over it and listened with flattering attention to everybody else's opinions without offering any of her own. She didn't hum even one song.

Jesse, to the surprise of everyone, emerged from the sanctuary of the sun porch to join us. His reddish hair was still wet from an early morning shower and his mustache stuck out at the ends. He'd had no personal contact with Stubb Flanders, but he expounded at length on the part divine intervention might have played in Stubb's strange death. When he got bogged down by the fact that divine intervention and murder would likely be incompatible, he gave up and invited Lee Lee to see his latest sculpture-in-progress.

Around ten, when Maggie still hadn't come downstairs, Amy took up some coffee and left it beside her bed.

I was grateful that our names hadn't been listed in any of the newspaper accounts and was about to say so when the phone rang and a woman from the sheriff's department asked if I could drive out to Lost River to identify the pictures on my camera. I agreed, hoping that meant I'd get it back afterward.

Lee Lee, after inspecting Jesse's pots and sculptures, asked if she could tag along, and at eleven I dropped her in front of St. Jude's and drove on to the sheriff's substation.

Again I braved the bulletproof mirror and spoke to the invisible dispatcher behind it. Her microphone-enhanced voice told me to have a seat, and a couple of minutes later, Detective Christensen appeared and led the way to his office. Yesterday, I couldn't have said what he looked like, but today I noticed. His hair was cut short and would probably have been curly if he'd let it grow. He was fortyish, with alert, brown eyes and creases in his face that suggested a dry sense of humor when he wasn't on duty.

He'd transferred my photos to a laptop computer, and they were damned good pictures, if I say so myself. He scrolled quickly through a hundred or more time-coded snaps but was most interested in the ones of Candy Butler walking around the church to find Stubb. He also asked about the guys sitting at the picnic table.

"We'd like to talk to them, hear what they saw that night, but we haven't been able to locate them. Your friend Luane agrees with you that they never left the table." He shifted in his chair. "Another witnesses, a woman who was standing around in front of the church, saw them arrive around nine. She said they smelled like onions. Did you notice that, Mrs. Shaw?"

"I never got that close."

"But they were the same three guys you saw in," he glanced down at his notes, "the Whole Hog Saloon the night before?"

"I think so, but they were wasted and one was asleep on the table."

Christensen asked a few more questions, then leaned back in his chair, studying my face.

"So," he said finally, "if we believe the newspapers, a bunch of people were watching the front of the church, Mr. Flanders was watching the back and side of the church, and everybody else was watching everybody else. Since none of the windows open wide enough to let anybody in and nobody went near any of the doors, Mr. Flanders either offed himself or it was another damned miracle. Any idea how we might find the three guys at the picnic table?"

"Me?" I shook my head. "The bartender at the Whole Hog Saloon must know them. Or some of the people walking around the church."

The detective raised both palms from the desk in a helpless gesture. "Not that easy, Ms. Shaw. Not everybody's a model citizen like you. Lot of things happen in small towns — murder, rape, robbery — we may know who was responsible, but it's always a question of proof. Unless somebody comes into the station and says 'I did it,' sometimes we're out of luck. You know," he said, leaning back in his chair, "you'd make a good suspect yourself."

I stared at him. "I never moved from the front of the church. A lot of people saw me sitting there all night long."

He nodded slowly. "But what if you arranged to have people out front for an alibi? People who'd swear themselves blue you never left your chair?"

I didn't bother keeping the sarcasm out of my voice. "Like the Boy Scouts? Don't they all swear to tell the truth, or were they just short friends in disguise?"

He leaned back in his chair. "I'm just saying. It's all hypothetical at this point. Trying to figure out what happened."

I was not cheerful when I left the substation without my camera, and my mood didn't improve when I discovered Candy Butler propped against the hood of my car.

She didn't bother saying hello, just jumped right in with both hand-tooled boots.

"Thought maybe you'd like to come out to the ranch for lunch. I've got a really good cook."

"How'd you know I was here?" When I'm tired, my voice can be curt to the point of nasty.

"Called your house. Wanted to talk to you about a couple of things."

I shook my head. "I have to get home. Anyway, there's somebody with me. Lee Lee, the girl you met last night. She's at the church. I can't just leave her there."

She threw up her hands. "Pick the girl up and bring her too. It's lunch, for God's sake, and there's no place to talk in this town without everybody seeing and hearing everything that goes on. You can drive your own car and leave whenever you want, okay? Follow me."

Ms. Butler hopped in her Range Rover, which was parked next to the BMW, ran through the gears and waited for me to obey.

I let her sit while I thought about it, then got in my car and drove down the street to the church where Lee Lee was waiting in line for the dirt room. She said the police tape would be removed within the hour and she couldn't wait to experience the healing earth, but if I was in a hurry to get home, she could maybe find another ride. That and the fact I was hungry and too tired to think about it, decided it. I said I'd be back in an hour or so, and she nodded happily and resumed her conversation with a guy tattooed from the top of his bald head to the nape of his neck.

The Butler Ranch, eight miles out of town, was pasture and palmettos and scrub pine as far as you could see. The house sat half a mile off the main road at the end of a white gravel driveway behind fancy black iron gates with a push button entry. There was a lot of white painted fence surrounding a cluster of pale yellow buildings: a barn, several stables, and other structures I couldn't put a name to.

Candy Butler's cook/housekeeper served us grilled chicken, saffron rice and a sauce that tasted like oranges and limes and garlic.

Candy began speaking her mind the minute we sat down at the table and continued speaking it around mouthfuls of chicken and rice and sweet tea.

"The police are going after me on this one," she assured me. "Which is plain stupid. I might have blown a hole in his backside, but I wouldn't go to jail for a slug like Stubb Flanders."

"Why would they pick on you?" I barely suppressed a yawn. "You're a respectable citizen, a landowner, not somebody who goes around murdering people."

There was a small, uncomfortable silence, then she let out her breath in a whoosh. "The problem is St. Jude's security system. If they can prove somebody knew the code, that's who they're going to pin it on. And they'll think Father Mike gave it to me. But he didn't."

"Why would they think he did?"

"Father and I are close friends, have been for years." Her voice faded a bit at the end of the sentence.

I raised an eyebrow.

"No, no, nothing like that," she said impatiently. "In fact, he's still furious with me about the brochure." She ran a hand through her curly black hair. "The thing is, I was there when they installed the system."

Eating lunch had made me even more tired, and I was finding it hard to follow. "What does that mean, exactly?"

"I'm *trying* to tell you!" she snapped. "I was *there* when they put it in and told Father to enter his own secret code number. I know it's a joke, but he kept it just the way it came from the factory: one, two, three, four. He thought it was the last thing anybody would expect. And it was. It worked fine for the past fourteen years."

"Anybody else have the code? An assistant, aide, volunteer?"

She shook her head. "Father Mike opens the front doors every morning, leaves after the midday mass and comes back to lock up just before seven p.m. There are volunteers who stick around afternoons, but none of them have keys or numbers."

I shrugged. "Well, I can see you may have a problem, but why tell me about it?"

"Because you knew Stubb Flanders before, from a long time ago, the kind of guy he was. I want you to check out his enemies. I don't think this is a Lost River thing. Most likely somebody from his past killed him. I want to find out what really happened before the police get too sure about anything."

"Then hire somebody to check it out," I said, irritably. "I can't do that."

"Sure you can. You did it in England last summer."

"But that wasn't . . . Where did you hear about that?"

"I know people who know people." She stared at me across the table. "They told me you solved a murder over there."

"Not exactly." I shifted uncomfortably in my chair. "It was a very old murder — way back in nineteen sixty-six — and nobody gave a damn, to put it bluntly, except a friend of mine. She needed to know what happened."

"Still, you did what she wanted. And you stopped somebody from murdering her too."

"That was different. Who told you all this?"

"Another friend of yours. Probably our next state representative."

Oh, hell, Tom Roddler. Damn Tom, anyway. I studied Candy Butter through narrowed eyes and decided she wasn't enough his type, either age or looks wise, to get him talking.

"What is it you've got on Tom?"

"Nothing." Ms. Butler held out both hands, palms up. "I know somebody who knows him, is all. I also know about the murders you figured out in Seminole Beach — the kid on drugs, and that one back in the forties."

When I didn't respond, her chin went up and she looked annoyed. "It's not like I expect you do this for free, you know. I pay my —"

She broke off as I opened my mouth to protest.

"And don't tell me you don't need the money right now. That's what Tom said you'd say. But that's just stupid. You know what Dolly Parton says: 'Ain't nobody got so much money they don't want all the money that's coming to them.' "

Dolly Parton? I raised a hand to stop the flow.

"Ms. Butler, we're not talking some kind of hobby here. I got involved in the forties thing by accident, and I went to London partly as a favor to Tom. Both times I was very, very lucky, but it wouldn't have made any difference if I'd failed. If you're seriously concerned about being arrested, you need professional help, not an outsider who makes things worse. The police are all over this. They won't like it if somebody pokes around in their business."

"You're right, they won't." Candy Butler put her elbows on the table and rested her chin on her hands. "So what if I just hire you to find my missing kid, Bobby? How about that? That doesn't step on any toes. And in the meantime, if you happen to stumble across any useful information . . ."

"Your son?" I shook my head. "You've lost me completely.

I don't know anything about missing persons. Wouldn't know where to start."

She rolled right over me. "Right here, of course. He grew up in Lost River from seven on. Some of his teachers are still around, retired now. I've got some pictures that might help. And a police report that says nothing much."

"But, good Lord, if the police couldn't find him . . . he could be anywhere in the country — maybe not even in the country."

"I don't expect you to *find* him. Just pretend to be looking. Check around, see what you come up with. Two birds with one stone. Tom Roddler says you've got a gift for uncovering secrets. He says it's a kind of psychic thing."

At the look on my face, she laughed. "I know, I know. Tom wouldn't know psychic if it bit him in the ass, but he believes you do something that makes the truth come out."

I looked her over again, reassessing the possibility that she and Tom had ever had a fling. Tom has a habit of doing favors for his women friends. Even when it means throwing previous women friends under the bus.

Over dessert, a three-cream cake as good as anything Amy makes, Candy Butler produced another surprise: a quarter inch thick, expertly typed report on Stubb Flanders: his birth in London, his parents' death in an automobile accident, the aunt who raised him, now dead. His whole Bolivian fiasco was covered, along with his connection to Maggie Gilchrist and a slighter one to me. The front cover was missing, so it was impossible to tell who had generated the report or when. However, it ended when Stubb moved out of Maggie's New York apartment and left no forwarding address.

"I've got somebody working on the missing stuff," Ms. Butler said, as if she'd read my mind.

I looked back down at the report for a couple of minutes. Then I put it down and held out my hand.

"What?" She looked blank.

"Let's see the one you had done on me."

Chapter 8

Ms. Butler stared at my open hand for maybe three seconds, flashed me a smile that was pleased more than anything else, and disappeared into the next room.

My report was thinner than Stubb's and was just basic background, nothing to make you squirm, but aggravating all the same. It covered college transcripts, my years as a photojournalist in Europe, my marriage and move to Seminole Beach, the years teaching at the college, my ex-husband's death six hours after our divorce was final, the house on 32 River Road, the names and ages of my renters, the names of a few close personal friends, notably Tom Roddler, and details of my last trip to England.

I closed the report and fanned myself slowly with it. "According to the date, you got a full report two days after we met,"

I said with a mean smile. "You have a hacker on your payroll?"

Candy Butler shrugged. "I like to know my enemies — and friends. You showed up at the church with that asshole Flanders. I wanted to know why."

I flipped through Stubb's file again. "I see Mr. Flanders' report is typed, rather than computer generated. How long ago was it done — ten, twelve years maybe?"

For a second she didn't answer, then gave me a long hard look. "You're smarter than you look, but that's good because I need you to be. I think this murder's gonna to be right up your alley, some old connection out of Flander's past — nothing to do with me, really. But the problem is, if the police find out how well I knew him — put that when they find out — they're not gonna to look far back. They're gonna nail me for sure, whether I lawyer-up or not." She let out a whoosh of air. "I had the report done after that botched-up mess in Bolivia. Stubb Flanders headed up a team of journalists and photographers, and that team included two brothers: Bobby and Scott McCleod. Do you remember the story at all?"

"Sure. Somebody died."

"Four people died. One was Scott McCleod. Scott and Bobby were my sons, twins from my first marriage. Bobby's the one that dropped out of sight. The one you can pretend to be looking for."

Pretend to be looking for? That was a strange way to put it. I stayed silent, remembering the media coverage of Stubb's disastrous South American trip.

"It wasn't that I was going to *do* anything to the asshole," her hand swept the typed report aside. "I just wanted to know about him, what really happened. He killed Scott just like he put a gun to his head, and he should have killed Bobby too. Bobby never really had a life after Scott was gone."

I drew in a long breath. "How long's Bobby been missing?"

"Three, four years. He came back after his brother died, but he couldn't settle. Tried working the ranch for awhile, but he got into drugs and booze and whatever else was going. After awhile he just drifted away. He was in Lauderdale first, then some place in Montana, then Canada. I'd get a card saying he was off the stuff and getting straightened out and he'd be home soon. Then another one would come from California or New Mexico. After awhile, the cards stopped and so did the promises. Years of promises, and none of 'em ever . . ." Her mouth turned down at the corners. "Anyway, last time I heard, he was working on a ranch in Wyoming. There was even a rumor . . ." She hesitated and cleared her throat. "That he fell down a flight of stairs drunk and broke his neck a couple years back." She lifted her chin and almost managed to look like a suffering mother. "That's not true, either. He's out there somewhere. I know it."

She took a huge breath and made that whooshing sound again.

"Then Stubb Flanders shows up here — in my town and at my ranch. Out of nowhere. You think the police are going to believe that him being here is some big coincidence?"

"I can see why you're worried." I closed the report. "You hated Stubb, you knew the code to the church's security system and you were on the spot the night he was killed. Looking for him, you said."

"Looking to see what the hell he was up to." Her laugh was short and harsh." I don't have a prayer. Even my lawyer's not giving me any warm, fuzzy feedback, and he ought to be. He's made enough off me over the years."

"Get a different lawyer. Get a team of them."

She took in an impatient breath. "Like O.J.? I don't think so. I don't give a rat's ass what anybody says about me personally. The problem is, I'm fucking claustrophobic. Can't stand closed places, not even overnight. Sleep with the windows open when it's ninety degrees out. I'll go crazy if they lock me up. Have to hang myself, and I'm not doing that."

For a second, she actually seemed to have trouble getting her breath, then she slid her chair back so hard it squeaked on the wood floor.

"Look, I don't want to figure in this investigation at all, but they called me down to the station soon as they heard I'd been at the church, and then they came out here and went through damn near everything."

"They had a warrant?"

"No. They asked. Nicely. I figured, What the hell, there was nothing here to find, so I told them to go ahead. They took the clothes I was wearing at the church, for God's sake. We're not talking old-time lawmen, now. Lost River's not incorporated, so we get sheriff's deputies, college boys. They don't care who you are or if you carry any weight around town. They only want facts."

She pushed the chair again, stretched out her legs and crossed her ankles. "What I want you to do is talk to people, see if anything strikes you while you're listening to them. If you can solve a fifty-year-old murder, you can surely figure out what happened when you're Johnny on the spot." She reached in her pocket. "I gotta have a cigarette. Want one?"

I shook my head no.

She found a book of matches in her pocket and lit up.

"If you can't find anything," she blew a puff smoke straight out in front of her, "then I'll have to regroup."

"What about your son's father?" I said, humoring her. "Any possibility there?"

"No." She threw the matchbook down on the table. "Dead a long time. And he wouldn't avenge anybody, including himself, even if he was alive."

"The cleaning girl Stubb supposedly seduced?"

"Not supposedly, and again, no. And no to her father too. The man's a saint. Works his fingers to the bone for that family."

"The miracle boy, Andreas? Or his father? They were both pretty upset with Stubb."

"Nope." She blew out more smoke. "Anyway, they're not around. Went back to Guatamala two days after your Mr. Flanders tried to interrogate the boy. Probably won't be back." She sighed. "Even I can see I'm the best hope the cops have."

"But," I said, frowning, "even if you knew the alarm code, somebody would've seen you enter the church. There's no door in the back, and at least three people besides me can testify you never went near the front doors. The windows on both sides of the church only open about six, seven inches." I glanced at her mid section. "No offense, but you couldn't squeeze through a six-inch space on a bet. And there were three guys on the picnic table facing the side door. They'd have noticed if you tried to get in that way."

Candy Butler decided not to be insulted. "Then that's what you do first," she said in a business-like tone. "Find those three guys. Find out how drunk they were and what they actually did see."

By the time I went out to my car, I was still uncommitted, although Ms. Butler hadn't stopped pushing for an answer. As I opened my car door, a guy on horseback came trotting up to the house. He looked like the Marlborough Man, only Central

Florida style. Denim jeans, roll-sleeved khaki shirt, cowboy hat. He was on the good side of fifty and whoever wrote "mean and lean" must have had him in mind when they wrote it.

Candy Butler introduced him as Pete Beck, her foreman, and he pulled off his sunglasses, said "Ma'am," and looked straight into my eyes for a couple of seconds. Then he said something about a sick mare, and she told him she'd be there in a minute. The horse turned and moseyed back toward one of the barns. The foreman replaced his sunglasses and kind of moseyed too.

"Always something," Ms. Butler muttered. She gave me a wave, jumped into her Jeep and followed her hired man.

"Whew," I said to nobody in particular. "No wonder she's so into ranching."

On the way out of town, I picked up Lee Lee, who was in some kind of exalted state after her session with the healing earth. She carried a small paper bag of the stuff but didn't want to discuss it, which suited me fine. I was grateful for the silence. Why was Ms. Butler so determined to hire me? And why the hell had Tom given her my name? There was a time when I'd have called him up and asked, but not now. As I said, Tom can talk anybody into anything. My mind strayed into forbidden territory for a moment, then back to Candy Butler. Why would she want me rummaging around in the events surrounding Stubb's murder?

Because the more people involved in Stubb's death, my tired mind responded, *particularly somebody who knew him long ago, the less the police will look at her.*

I tightened my grip on the steering wheel and rolled down my window. Air cold enough to make me shiver created a wind tunnel inside the car, but I didn't care. If Ms. Butler was that twisty, maybe turning her down flat wasn't in my best interest.

People with a lot of money don't usually go to jail if there's somebody else to pin it on. Bear, Amy, Kenji and I had been at the church much longer than Ms. Butler on the night of the murder. Stubb had spent a night in my house, and Maggie Gilchrist was currently sleeping in Room Number Three. Both Stubb's past and present seemed to lead directly to me and my friends at 32 East River Road.

Amy looked more than relieved when Lee Lee and I walked in the kitchen. Maggie was up, sitting at the worktable over a cup of coffee she obviously hadn't poured herself. Lee Lee muttered a quick hello and disappeared in the direction of the stairs, apparently to think some more about dirt.

I stayed in the kitchen against my will. I didn't know what to say to Maggie, either, and she was obviously in tough shape. Still, she was my friend, so I dutifully hunted up a pair of flip flops to replace the Ferragamo sandals on her feet and drove her out to the beach for a walk.

It had warmed up to the mid-seventies, warm enough not to need a jacket, with a light breeze and waves foaming in on the shore. A lot of other people were walking, too, but they were clearly having a much better time than we were.

Maggie stumbled along in the sand, oblivious to the waves, the people or the glittering sun.

I decided the best thing to do was just walk her until she complained, but we'd probably done a couple of miles before she even raised her head.

Then she looked at me blankly and said. "Are we going somewhere?"

I nodded and turned us around. "Just a little farther."

A few hundred yards back up the beach, we climbed wooden

steps leading to the dune crossover and entered a restaurant called The Clam Strip. There were lots of people sitting at the long tiki bar, but one of the umbrella tables on the patio was free. I herded her in that direction.

She didn't respond when the waitress asked if we wanted a drink, but when I ordered a Bloody Mary, she blinked a couple of times, so I took a chance and ordered two. Two blinks, yes? One blink, no? For one blindingly grateful moment, I was glad I'd never had children. I'm not hard wired to deal with people needier than me.

"Okay, Maggie," I leaned across the table toward her. "I know this is horrible. I know nothing's going to make you feel better for a long, long time. But I want to know what was going on with Stubb."

Her voice was lifeless. "Why? You never liked him to start with."

"True. I thought he was a first-class jerk. Everything he touched got damaged, you included."

"If you're saying he was a wanker at times, I know that." She stopped talking as the girl appeared with our order.

"I never heard that one before," the waitress remarked, putting down our drinks. "What's a wanker?"

"It's British for dickhead," I said, and she walked away, laughing.

Maggie frowned at the big, grilled shrimp hanging off the rim of her Bloody Mary. "I know he could be a wanker," she said in a dull voice," but you never saw the other side of him. The side that really needed somebody to care about him. Nobody did. All that . . . stuff . . . he did was really . . . really just . . ."

"Let me guess, a cry for help?"

"No! You're like everybody else. People aren't one dimensional, Keegan. I've seen the real Stubb dozens of times. I've seen him . . . I've seen him cry . . ." A dry sob broke up the words, and she put both hands up to her eyes. "I was the only one who ever . . . the only one he came to when he was in trouble. He said he was a better person when he was with me."

I didn't even touch that. I swallowed some of my drink and stirred it for awhile with the celery stalk.

"I don't know anything about him after that — mess — in South America," I finally said. "I heard he left the U.K. and went to New York but that he left there too."

"He had to leave London." Maggie removed the shrimp, the celery, the skewered olive and lime from her drink and piled them on a napkin. She drank down a couple of inches of her drink.

"They all blamed him — everybody. It wasn't his fault if a bunch of drug dealers shot everybody. He was almost killed himself." She shook her head angrily. "One of the photographers, Bobby McCleod, told an interviewer that Stubb was a drunk and a coward and had sold the rest of them out. Just because they didn't actually hit him with a bullet doesn't mean he was a coward and ran away. He didn't. But Bobby was so bitter about his brother's death he had to blame somebody. What did they want Stubb to do? Not run? Stay around and be shot too? It's no wonder he drank."

Good God, I thought, *the old Maggie never contradicted herself, ever, let alone twice in the same paragraph.* And she must have read the same reports as the rest of the world. My former best friend was living large in denial land.

I studied her across the table. Same long, reddish hair combed smooth from a center part, same gray-green eyes. But she was probably fifteen pounds thinner than the last time I'd seen her, her skin was pinched and white, and there were wrinkles around her mouth. Dissatisfaction with her life in general or just dry skin? Maggie was two years younger than me and had zero interest in family life when I knew her. But when you got older and tired of being alone, sometimes that changed.

"Tell me about Stubb," I said again, waving at the girl for another drink. "What did he do in New York? Who did he work for?"

Maggie's shoulders slumped even further. "Nothing and nobody, as far as I know. A couple of years after he moved, he wrote me in London. He'd run through what money he had by then."

I reached over and picked up her discarded shrimp. "And?"

"There was a job in New York and I flew over to interview for it — and got it — and found an apartment . . ."

"And Stubb moved in with you." I finished for her.

"Well, he couldn't find work. Not the kind of work he was used to doing, and he was so depressed . . ." She drained the rest of her drink and started defoliating the new one. "We were doing all right, and then he just left. Disappeared one day. Didn't write, didn't call. I hired a detective agency to find him, and they reported him in more places than Elvis. They did actually find him tending bar in New Orleans, before Katrina, and I flew down there to see him. He said he wasn't fit company to be around and didn't want to do that to me but was getting himself together and promised to call in a couple of months. He didn't, of course, and then the hurricane hit."

"You didn't hear from him after that?"

She shook her head. "Years without a word. It's hard to . . . there's nobody out there, really . . . I mean, you meet people, but it's like your life's on hold."

"And then he turned up again." It wasn't a question, but she answered it that way.

"Yes. He wanted us to try it again. He was determined to make it work and to find a photography gig, so I helped him. A friend of mine was editing a new online magazine and did me a favor. Somebody sent Stubb a brochure about this miracle earth thing, and he got really gung-ho about it. He was just to fly down here, shoot pictures of Lost River and St. Jude's, and write up the story. That's all it was supposed to be, a chance to get his foot back in the door. But he got this — thing about the dirt in his head — that bringing it in made it a scam. It didn't even make sense, but he wouldn't listen."

"Any idea how he planned to expose it?"

"Not really. He said the miracle cure wasn't a cure at all; that the boy should have been diagnosed as electively mute. And he was furious when the priest wouldn't let him shoot pictures of the dirt itself." She paused. "There was something about the priest, something Stubb found out from an old journalist friend. He said Father Mike would be in a boatload of trouble if he didn't start being more agreeable."

"Did he say what kind of trouble?"

Maggie shook her head. "But it wasn't about anything that happened down here." She picked up her drink again. "He refused to do any color or background at all and he hated inland Florida. Said it was hell surrounded by cane fields. Some days he was so wired. You know Stubb, when he wasn't drinking, he lived on caffeine. Chugged Red Bull all day long."

Her face changed suddenly and she put down the glass, propped her elbows on the table and let her forehead rest in her hands. "Oh, God. What am I going to do?"

"Thank your lucky stars" didn't seem like the right answer

at this point. I wondered if years of dealing with Stubb, or the absence of Stubb, had caused more problems than simply heartache. Like clinical depression maybe? The old Maggie would have kicked a guy like Stubb Flanders to the curb the first time he came looking for free rent.

My thoughts came to a stop as she straightened up, checked her watch and said, "I need the loo." She was up and gone before I could tell her where it was.

When she came back, she'd washed her face, touched up her makeup, particularly around the eyes, and looked calmer. She sat down, hooked her thin, flat shoulder bag over the back of the stool and flagged down a waitress. She ordered a scotch and looked a question at me. I shook my head. "I'm driving."

"Bring two anyway," Maggie told the girl and forced a twisted smile. "It's happy hour."

Chapter 9

By the time we drove back to the house, it was nearly dinner time, and Maggie was feeling no pain. Amy was experimenting with some dish that was supposedly a smash hit in Madagascar. It looked like baby octopus nesting in shredded raw artichokes and tasted like sweat socks. Hopefully, some variation of it wouldn't turn up in her latest cookbook.

Nobody ate with enthusiasm, but nobody complained. Like me, they remembered the two grim months Amy had been in New York, months when everyone cooked for themselves and the kitchen was a culinary wasteland of greasy, piled-high pans. I closed my eyes and pretended the white rubbery stuff was cauliflower. It's easier to swallow something with legs if you think it's a vegetable.

Only Jesse and Lee Lee finished their dinner. Everybody

else concentrated on Madagascar's national drink, large pitchers of green pepper rum. In fact, everyone focused so hard, it was awhile before I realized Maggie was focusing harder than anyone else.

Even Bear, who puts away vast amounts of liquor without feeling the effect, noticed Maggie's intake. Surprisingly, he didn't say anything, and Bear can be brutal. Instead, he questioned me about my trip to Lost River earlier in the day.

I told him about Candy Butler's offer, her twin boys and the reports she'd had done on Stubb and me. Also about her suggestion that I search for the missing son as a cover for investigating Stubb's past.

Bear looked surprised. "Why not hire some heavy hitters out of Miami? I mean, no offense, but why ask you?'

I shrugged. "She *claims* it's because I was recommended by an old friend and is convinced I have ESP. I think she's an extremely devious woman who's legitimately worried about herself and reckless on top of it. She acts on impulse and deals with the fallout later."

"Are you going to work for her?"

"Probably not. Anyway, I hate poking in other people's business — appearances to the contrary."

"Should go to detective school," Kenji suggested, "if you are going to . . . investigate things."

"Listen to Kenji." Amy stood and started picking up plates. "Last time you stuck your nose in something, two guys tried to throw you off a bridge."

Bear studied me from across the table. "Maybe she's just tossing you into the mix to give the police something extra to do. They'll be busy checking out everybody who was within ten feet of the crime. Where they live, who their friends are, which ones they've slept with, where they went to school, whether they've ever been in St. Jude's before. By the time they finish, there won't be anything they don't know about Candy Butler — never mind you, the three of us, Lee Lee and the freaking Boy Scouts."

"I think you can skip the Scouts. They've already blown town."

Bear shook his head. "What I'm saying is, if she's as crafty as you think, maybe we should do some investigating on our own — just for protection. Although she's still the best bet. Even she admits she's the only one with a motive."

"That we know about," I agreed.

Lee Lee's usual sunny expression had faded as she listened to the discussion. But just as she opened her mouth to speak, Maggie Gilchrist, who was seated next to her, knocked over a glass of green pepper rum and slid gracefully out of her chair to the floor.

Bear got up, flashed me a long-suffering look and tried to get Maggie to her feet. When that didn't work, he levered her over one shoulder and carried her out of the dining room and up to her bedroom. I tossed my napkin on the table to stop the flow of rum and followed, but Bear had already deposited her on the floor when I got there.

He looked down his nose at me. "At the risk of sounding redundant, just leave her there. She'll only throw up in the bed."

Unfortunately, I didn't follow his advice, and he was correct, she did throw up. Several times. In the night. And since she was my friend, I was the one who cleaned up the mess and sat by the bed to make sure she kept her head turned sideways and didn't swallow her own vomit.

Around eight the next morning I showered away a profound lack of sleep, filled the BMW with two-dollar-a-gallon gas and headed for Lost River. On the way, I stopped downtown at Spike O's coffee shop for a latte and a newspaper.

Spike O's has the best coffee in town, as well as the most interesting clientele. The regulars call it Psycho's because a local psychologist used to hold court there after work, chatting and dispensing free therapy to anyone who wandered by. After a couple of years she moved to Sedona, but the name stuck.

I checked the front page of the *Sentinel*. Some gung-ho reporter had dug out the story of Stubb Flanders' Bolivian screwup and given it the same reporting treatment as his death. There were paragraphs full of dark jungle shadows, vicious drug barons, wily killers and enough colorful adjectives to choke a linguist. When you got through the drama, the facts were:

In 1994, Stubb Flanders became the youngest photographer ever to have a picture named World Press Photo of the Year.

In 1995, he topped that with a *Newsweek* cover story on pyramid schemes.

In 1996, he led a team of other photojournalists, including the up-and-coming McCleod brothers, into a Bolivian jungle to cover a story on mobile cocaine laboratories. They ran into a turf battle between cartels, Flanders got away, and the rest were reported killed. For a couple of weeks, Stubb was a staple on news and talk shows as he promoted his soon-to-be-published book, cleverly titled, *Escape from the Drug Lords*.

Weeks later, two members of the photography team, one of them Bobby McCleod, turned up in La Paz with an entirely different story and eventually went before the CPJ (Committee to Protect Journalists), charging that Flanders was a drunk and a coward who led the rest of them into a trap, then fled.

It was a depressing story, and now that I knew what had happened to Bobby McCleod, it was more so. I quit reading and turned to the comics. Poor Maggie. Attachment to an asshole for umpteen years was bad enough; attachment to an inept asshole was the stuff of tragedy.

I dragged my tired body and a second cup of coffee out of the coffee shop and into the BMW. Sometime during the night, between bouts of paper-toweling throw up, I had decided to take a few days and poke around Lost River. Partly, I was doing it because I thought Bear was right and I wanted to stop Candy Butler from ordering dossiers on everybody I knew — including a more extensive one on me. (Real dirt isn't hard to find if you keep looking.) Partly, I wanted to know how Stubb got in the church without setting off the alarm. But mostly, I was doing it to get out of the house. I didn't know how to deal with an old friend who was drinking too much and tap dancing on the verge of a mini-breakdown.

I pulled out my cell phone and punched in Candy Butler's number. When I got her voice message, I told it I'd spend a couple of days on her problem, see what I could find out, and we could talk further. Then I reviewed the short to-do list I'd made around three that morning. First, speak to Father Mike, the priest at St. Jude's, for particulars about the alarm system. Second, interview the girl who cleaned the church, the one Stubb had supposedly date-raped. Third, visit a woman called Meyerson — the only teacher Candy Butler could remember — who'd taught Bobby McCleod in eighth grade. I wasn't really looking for him, but it wouldn't hurt if that story got around Lost River. Any information about Candy Butler would be enlightening, and Mrs. Meyerson was likely an expert on her student's moms.

Father Mike's house was a white cinder block, built in the seventies, with a minimalist front yard and a dark green front door. I hadn't called ahead, but I remembered what Candy Butler told me about his schedule.

Father Mike answered the door himself, and if he hesitated an instant before inviting me in, it was gracefully done. I didn't blame him. He looked older this morning, a little grim and gray faced, but twenty years of weekending in Lost River might do that to you. Never mind a murder in the back room of your church.

There was a lot of old fashioned, painted bamboo furniture in his den, and he motioned me to a chair that rocked.

"You don't have a camera today," he remarked, with a slight smile. I thought he was torn between ministering to a woman whose friend had been murdered and avoiding a woman who was probably trouble.

"No, the police took it. They thought it might be evidence." I leaned forward in the rocker. "First, Father, I'm sorry Stubb was . . . fixated on the dirt-level thing. People tried to tell him it was a non-issue and that nobody claimed the earth replenished itself, but he wouldn't listen. He had several copies of that old brochure Ms. Butler wrote and was only interested in his own interpretation."

Father Mike made a noise in his throat. "It's unfortunate. These extravagant claims for St. Jude's earth. The presence of the media in what was always a personal miracle. And now, this terrible thing . . ."

His alert, intelligent eyes shifted from one of the jalousie windows to meet mine. "I'm sorry for the loss of your colleague. What can I do for you, Mrs. Shaw?"

I decided to skip Candy Butler's cover story and stick to the truth without too many details.

"I'm not sure, Father. Ms. Butler found out I'd been involved in a couple of — well, investigations — and wants to hire me. She thinks the sheriff's department will try to pin Stubb's death on her. She had a run-in with him when he first came to town, and she claims she knows the code for the alarm system. Her idea is that I pretend to be looking for her son Bobby, who disappeared years ago. while I really try to find out what happened to Stubb."

His eyebrows rose. "And you've agreed to do that?"

I shook my head. "I'm not an investigator and I told her so. I did finally say I'd ask some questions, check around a little."

"She's a persuading sort of women," Father Mike agreed, "or are you looking for reasons of your own?" A smile lit his somber face. "Ah, I see. You're starting with me. Is that it?"

"I guess so. I did wonder about the alarm. Stubb Flanders had no way of knowing the access code. Is it possible somebody hid in the church and turned it off? Let him in later?"

"No." He paused for a second. "Just so we're clear, are you preparing an article of some sort? Newspaper? Magazine? Television? A blog?"

"No. The thing is, Father, I drove Stubb Flanders out to the church, and I was there, out front all night. I'm trying to understand how he died . . ." I heard my own words die away, with a forlorn tone I hadn't intended, but before I could regroup, the priest was talking again.

"Understood. I check all three back rooms every night before I lock up. And walk down through the pews. There's no other place to hide."

I nodded.

"The alarm system is interior only and isn't motion sensitive. We didn't need something to guard against theft, only incursion. You press a number code on the keypad before you leave the building, which arms the system. If anyone opens a door or window without disarming it, a siren goes off, and a phone calls goes to the monitoring company. You have two minutes to enter the disarming code after you open the door."

"Is the code written down, filed away anywhere?"

"Just in my brain."

"And you and Ms. Butler are the only people who know the numbers."

He sat farther back in his chair. "I can't speak for anyone but myself. I have not personally entrusted the combination to anyone."

"Still, Stubb and somebody else managed to get into the church without setting off the alarm."

He nodded. "If I knew how it was done, I would certainly share the information with the police."

"You've been at St. Jude's a long time, Father. Twenty years?"

"Yes."

"Ever meet Stubb Flanders anywhere before? Like up north or at any other place you lived?"

For the first time I thought he looked uncomfortable, and his voice sharpened.

"Not to my knowledge. Are you seeing me as a suspect then, Mrs. Shaw?"

I shook my head. "Of course not. I just thought your paths might have crossed. And I was wondering why you stayed here so long. Don't priests get moved around pretty often?"

"They're allowed to stay put occasionally — if the space is available."

"And you like it here? It's pretty small, not a lot to do."

He lifted an eyebrow. "Lost River is where I need to be for now."

"Okay," I nodded and stood up. "One more thing. About the cures, is the healing earth anything like stigmata — those statues of Christ that suddenly start seeping blood? Is it actually a miracle or just a self-fulfilling belief?"

Father Mike rose to his feet, his face thoughtful. "There is always an official position and a popular position," he said slowly, "but there are only two real possibilities: divine action or demonic action. It may look like divine experience, but it's very possibly a deception. Paul says, second Corinthians, eleven, that Satan himself often comes dressed as an angel of the light."

"But Lost River is consecrated ground, isn't it? Because of the mission built here hundreds of years ago and also by eighty years of masses said in the church? How could it be a deception?"

"Messages may be tainted, and the information that goes out to the world will reflect that taint."

"But the boy, Andreas, was not himself deceptive?"

"No, but Andreas has other problems besides speech, and children are easily confused. Particularly children with limited experience of the world."

"Yet, you're not prepared to say the healing earth *doesn't* work miracles?"

Father Mike tilted his head. "The official position is always to stand back, evaluate and wait until it's finished. Are you a Catholic, Mrs. Shaw?"

I grinned at him and headed for the door. I know an exit cue when I hear one.

On the way to the car, I wondered what Stubb had discovered about Father Mike's past. Whichever deadly sin was involved, it must have been a lulu if it still worried the man after twenty years.

Candy Butler had given me Gail Meyerson's address the day we had lunch, and I tackled her next. She lived on the opposite side of town in a new-looking double-wide trailer. A golf cart was parked behind a red Volkswagen convertible in her driveway. Mrs. Meyers was tan, sun-wrinkled and probably eighty-plus. She was dressed in bright yellow Capri pants and a white T-shirt that proclaimed, "Tout comprendre, c'est tout pardoner."

I scrambled thorough my limited French. *All is understood, all is forgiven?* You'd probably need several shirts like that if you tried to make a living teaching eighth grade.

Mrs. Meyerson remembered Bobby McCleod clearly. "Wonderful boy," she said over a cup of coffee on her glassed-in porch. "Wonderful student. A very kind boy, which doesn't happen often at that age. Twelve, you know, very iffy at twelve. Good history student, cared about what was going on in the world. I was surprised when he became a journalist, he seemed more like the veterinarian type to me.

"Now, his brother, Scott, was a different story. He was an adventurer, always getting in trouble, driving too fast, falling out of cars. He even learned to fly his mother's plane. Scott was the kind of boy you'd expect to trek off into the jungle looking for a big story."

She stopped talking and slid a plate of cookies in my direction.

"Chocolate peppermint snaps, made them myself," she said, proudly. "Anyway, they both ended up at journalism school in Gainesville, for whatever reason. Twins, I guess. And they were both doing well, although I don't suppose they were making much money at it. And then . . . well, disaster."

I nodded and reached for another cookie.

"Anyway, it was all over the news at the time. They joined up with that English photographer, the one who's caused so much trouble about St. Jude's. And the next thing you know, Scott's been killed in the jungle on some secret assignment, and Bobby's back here alone. He couldn't settle to anything, and I thought at the time he should have had some help. Counseling or something like that, but his mother's the kind who thinks you should tough it out, no matter what the situation."

Mrs. Meyerson hesitated, started to say something else and decided against it. A deep frown creased her already wrinkled forehead. "That's been her life experience, anyway, and I guess it worked for her. After awhile, Bobby just disappeared. Left town."

"You didn't see him after that? Or hear from him?"

"No," she shook her head. "Technically, he was off my radar once the boys went to Seminole Beach for high school. The only reason I kept track of him at all is because this is a small town, and everybody knows everybody else. You know how the school system is — no secrets there."

When I left Mrs. Meyerson, I was long on cookies and short on information, but she had given me one interesting idea. I passed right by Seminole Beach High on my way home, and it was a ten-minute job to stop and look for pictures of Candy Butler's twins. Given the time frame, they would have graduated in the mid-eighties. Some of their teachers and old friends should still be around, and the more people I talked to, the better.

You're not really looking for Bobby McCleod, remember? The voice in my head was firm, obviously trying to make a point.

That's right, I wasn't. I was just . . . doing what? Getting out of the house, avoiding Maggie and a lot of emotion I didn't want to deal with? Trying to protect myself? Whatever. I shrugged off the voice and phoned Candy Butler. Before I tackled the high school, I wanted to find the girl who cleaned the church.

This time, Ms. Butler answered her phone, and after warning me to tread carefully with the girl's parents, read off an address on the west side of the town. I found the house easily enough, but not the girl. I was also exceedingly tactful, but it didn't matter. The woman who answered the door did not speak English, she said in English, and understood none of my Spanish 101 vocabulary.

Frustrated, I drove back in the direction of Seminole Beach High. I was just pulling into the parking lot when my cell phone rang.

"Maggie's locked herself in her room," Amy blurted out, as soon as she heard my voice. "She won't come out and doesn't answer. Should I call nine one-one?"

Chapter 10

When I got home, Bear and Amy were standing outside Room Number Three, but neither of them had persuaded Maggie to open her door.

Bear offered to climb out one of the bay windows in Number Four, swing himself to the windowsill of Maggie's room and break a pane, but Amy ignored him.

"I've got keys somewhere," she muttered, "duplicates from the locksmith."

She disappeared downstairs, and I banged on the door of Number Three a few more times then got down on my knees and looked through the old-fashioned keyhole. All I could see was a small section of wood floor.

"You sure she's in there?" I said to Bear.

"No." Bear shrugged. "But she doesn't seem to be anywhere

else. You think she took sleeping pills or something?"

"Maybe after I left this morning. There couldn't have been much on her stomach. Not after last night."

Bear's blue eyes narrowed. "She threw up, right?

"Copiously."

"I told you."

Amy came back up the stairs with a ring full of newish-looking, brass keys. The fourth one turned the lock.

Maggie was on the bed, facing the wall and didn't move when the three of us entered the cold, silent room. Her clothes and belongings were scattered everywhere and the odor of throw up still hung in the room, although I'd scrubbed the rug with soapy water.

She was so still, her body so limp, she could have been dead.

I moved closer to the bed and patted the shoulder closest to me. "Maggie? What's going on?"

Her eyes were wide open, staring at nothing. Then her head moved a quarter of an inch, and I nearly jumped.

"Should we take her to Emergency?" Amy muttered at me.

Maggie apparently heard that. Her head moved again and she whispered, "Leave . . . me . . . alone."

I waved Bear out of the room, and under threat of a call to the EMTs, managed to get Maggie up and into the shower while Amy changed all of her bedding, including the pillow. But once back in her room, she refused to talk or move for the rest of the day.

Around ten p.m., as I tucked myself up with a blanket and pillows in the wicker chair to make sure she didn't jump out a window or slit her wrists during the night, I realized I was running seriously short on horizontal sleep. One night spent in front of St. Jude's Church in a folding chair, last night sitting up so Maggie didn't choke on her own vomit and yet again tonight. Tomorrow was likely to be an extremely sucky day.

To make matters worse, Maggie went to sleep and stayed that way, while I grew increasingly uncomfortable, irritable and antsy. When even two post-WWI mysteries failed to keep my attention and my own thoughts were boring me stiff, I went down to the mezzanine, pulled a dusty, beat up suitcase from the back of the closet and hauled it back up to Maggie's room. Even then, it was a long time before I opened it. There was old stuff in there. Bad stuff. Not as devastating as Pandora's Box, admittedly — or as destructive as the Ark of the Covenant — but stuff that took guts to look at. Who wants to confront past miseries, when it takes all your energy to hang on to the present?

Eventually, I snapped open the locks on the suitcase and stared at the contents. Ticket stubs, old arty black-and-white shots, presents, souvenirs, old shillings and coppers and ha'pennies, other stuff I'd never been able to throw away. I pulled out a stack of photos, circa nineteen ninety London. There, in glorious color, were Stubb Flanders, Maggie Gilchrist, Keegan Shaw and a drop dead gorgeous guy I had never managed to forget.

I must have fallen asleep reliving those pre-millennium years. When I opened my eyes, it was after eight in the morning, and Maggie was on her side facing me, eyes on the open suitcase at my feet.

"Going somewhere?" She was as pale as if she'd been locked in the basement for a month.

"Feeling better?" I said, keeping all sympathy out of my voice.

"No." Her eyes closed and she pulled her knees up to her chin.

"You need to get dressed and come downstairs for coffee and something to eat," I said. "If you don't, Bear will come up and get you and probably try to have you committed somewhere. You scared hell out of us yesterday."

"Sorry." It was an unrepentant mumble. "I just couldn't . . ."

"I'm not moving from this chair until you get up."

Even then, it was most of another hour before she pulled herself together and unwillingly followed me down to the kitchen.

Bear was there, talking to Amy. He tossed an assessing look at Maggie, then said to me, "Storm's hanging off the coast, wind's blowing about twenty miles an hour, and I'm thinking of taking a board to the beach. Want to come?"

"Sure. Can we take Maggie with us? Maybe give her a quick surfing lesson?"

Bear's blue eyes said, *Not a chance*, and I hurried on. "Then later, you and I can go out to Lost River and do a little investigating."

Bear's belief that he's a gifted detective warred with his desire not to get involved in Maggie's problems. Finally, he gave a short jerk of his neck. "If you think she's up to it."

"She's doing great," I assured him.

Maggie didn't say anything.

At the beach, the wind blew at a steady clip and the sun drifted in and out of huge cloud banks. Breakers broke in a white foam line a couple hundred yards out then roared in ferociously. Maggie looked pathetically thin and white in the bathing suit I'd talked her into wearing, and I felt almost guilty about turning Bear loose on her. But how bad could it be? If she got tired, she could quit. Anyway, Florida surfing isn't like those pictures you see of California or Hawaii. Usually, the biggest swells you get off our beach are two or three feet high, and your ride never lasts longer than thirty seconds.

Bear pushed his board out to get in a few decent-sized waves, while I spread out an old blanket and anchored all four corners with shoes and car keys.

Maggie hadn't fussed about having a surfing lesson, but she was so lethargic, I wasn't sure she had the energy to protest. I watched her as she sat on the blanket, head down, elbows on her knees, eyes closed. She hadn't said a word all the way out.

"Listen, Maggie," I finally said, "you're going to have to get some help with this . . ."

When she didn't answer, I repeated it louder, in case the wind was drowning me out.

"I know, I heard. I'm sorry. I just keep thinking it can't be true, and then I remember that I made him take this job, forced him into it . . ." She tried to blink away the tears, "If I'd been there . . . none of this would have happened." She flipped over, face down on the blanket, and I could almost feel the sobs shaking her back.

I hate it when English people cry. I start babbling.

"That's one of those pre-dawn ancient beliefs," I said, "*If I'm there, nothing bad can happen to the person I love.* You know it's not true, Maggie. There's nothing anybody —"

"It is true." Her voice was muffled by the folds of the blanket, thick with grief. "I should have been there, in the room with him, I could have stopped it . . ."

I told myself to shut up, actually did so, and patted her shoulder again, even though I'm not a shoulder patter. I'm also not good at commiseration or comfort. I sat there for a long time, feeling awkward and wishing myself anywhere else. After awhile, I think she fell asleep.

Bear cut his session way short; he was only out about an hour and a half before he came in and helped Maggie get into my wet suit. He walked her into the water, moving slowly in the direction of the breaking waves. She went readily, if not enthusiastically, and I figured she was happy to get away from me.

I watched them reach the spot Bear had chosen and remembered my first lesson last year. He'd taught me all the basic stuff: learning to watch waves, paddling out, flopping face down on the board, staying under the water when you pearled. After an hour, I was so exhausted I could barely walk or talk, but I was more in my body than I'd been for years.

Bear was amazingly patient, and Maggie's lesson was short. After fifteen minutes or so, he half-carried her back through the surf to the sand, got her out of the wet suit and told her to take it easy.

I dragged on the wet suit, picked up my board and left him to babysit. It was a little rough getting out, but the waves were cleaner and smoother than the last time I surfed. I caught a few dud waves, then a couple of good ones and finally a zinger that was so steady, I managed to stand up and stay up for eight, nine seconds. Pure bliss.

When I finally came in, Bear was packing up, and Maggie was twitching and shivering. In the, Jeep, she curled up in back with a blanket and went to sleep. Bear glanced over his shoulder at her then back at me. "She taking anything? Besides booze?"

"I don't know. She didn't when we used to work together."

"You're going to have to do something. Getting her off liquor would be a good start."

"Dandy idea, Doctor Feelgood. How the hell do I do that?"

"I could do it if I had the time. Which I don't. She needs to eat. Notice how she doesn't touch food, just moves it around? She's a mess. Totally. Maybe she needs to go to A.A."

"She'll refuse, I think." I looked over at him, considering. "I'll pay you a couple hundred a day if you can get her to stop and, you know, exercise or something."

His head snapped around. "You're shitting me. Why?"

"I told you. I owe Maggie. She doesn't have any family left, that I know about, and apparently no friends except Stubb. She needs help, and I don't think she's going to get it on her own. I don't think she can."

Bear gave me a long look. "Must be some gigantic favor she did you."

"It was." For a second my mind slipped to the suitcase of old photographs. "So, do we have a deal?"

He put his foot down on the gas and Amy's Jeep picked up a little speed. "I'll take it under advisement."

When we got home, Bear walked Maggie up to her bedroom, but I stayed in the kitchen. Kenji had downloaded my pictures from the night of the murder, printed them out and arranged them on Amy's work table. Several, piled in a neat stack, he dismissed with "Not good," but the rest he went over with me, making technical comments about light, lack of light, shading and so on.

When he finished, I lined the prints up chronologically, the way the police had done. They showed an almost hour-by-hour chronicle of the night Stubb was murdered — from our trek to the back of St. Jude's Church to the Boy Scouts rolling up their sleeping bags the following morning.

I was still studying a snap of the three farm workers on the picnic table when Amy got a bottle of Chianti out of the fridge and poured some for the three of us. She likes it when you bring the world into her kitchen. It's like all her best childhood memories: aunts, cousins, grandparents sitting around a huge table drinking wine and eating huge amounts of pasta and arguing at the top of their voices. Sometimes she forgets she moved out because all the noise was driving her crazy.

Bear came downstairs alone, a few minutes later, and helped himself to wine. He placed a half empty bottle of vodka on the table. "Only thing she had in her room. I looked around. We'll try it a week and see how it goes."

"Thanks, Bear," I said. I turned back to Kenji and held up the photo of the three field-workers. "I took a couple of close ups, but it's still hard to distinguish their features."

Kenji pulled his coarse, dark hair into a makeshift ponytails. "Yesss. Can be . . . enlarged . . . but so many shadows . . ."

"I know, take a stab at it anyway, if you don't mind."

I picked up the picture I'd taken of Lee Lee as she returned from her aborted attempt to talk to Stubb. In it, her breezy, free-to-be-me persona was gone. Instead, she looked slightly shocked.

Good old Stubb. Still in there pitching, making people miserable right up to the minute he died.

"That reminds me," I said to Amy. "Is Lee Lee still with us? I haven't seen her since dinner night before last."

"She came down last night for Chinese. But she's in Lost River today."

"Really? How'd she get there, walk?"

"She took my Jeep."

"You're kidding. You don't even know her. What if she never brings it back?"

Amy smirked at me. "Then I'll report it stolen and get newer and much better wheels."

Chapter 11

We had meatloaf for dinner that night. That's kind of Amy's cooking M.O.: strange and wonderful experimentation, followed immediately by serious comfort food.

Lee Lee had returned from Lost River with enough dirt stories to keep us entertained through the mashed potatoes, gravy and pan-fried sweet corn. She'd met all these people at the church, tons of them, she said, and although she was sure some of them were not really believers, just gawkers attracted by the bad publicity, she was confident that the healing room was strong enough to reverse any negative vibrations.

Jesse hung on every wacky word of her dinner monologue, but I was pleased to see he didn't look smitten. Jesse, when smitten, is best experienced sparingly. He looked pretty decent tonight, reddish hair combed, mustache trimmed, clothes only partially wrinkled. Maybe he'd get interested in his herb garden again, dig up all the plants that had gone to seed. The old Jesse had loved everything: his pots, the sunlight that glazed them when the porch windows were open, his mattress/bed on the box against the wall. In fact, he'd been so full of love for everything, I used to think he'd been released early from some place with barbed wire on top of the fence. But then he met a girl called Jerricha, and love for an actual human had nearly finished him.

Lee Lee thanked Amy effusively for the use of the Jeep and said she'd left gas money on the kitchen table. Apparently, she'd driven all over Lost River, exploring street after tiny little street. She loved the place, loved the people, but especially she loved the atmosphere.

"It's real Florida, you know? Cattle and horses and small town life. Like it used to be."

Bear rolled his eyes a couple of times but otherwise stayed quiet, keeping his attention on Maggie. She'd made it downstairs on time, but she looked like she'd slept in her clothes. She did manage to chew and swallow a few bites, but mostly she just shoved meatloaf around her plate.

After dinner, Kenji offered to help Amy with the dishes, and Jesse and Lee Lee took their coffee out on the sun porch to continue the magic earth discussion. I coaxed Maggie into a walk around the back yard.

"Isn't that what you Brits do after dinner?" I said to her. "Show guests your gardens? In the UK, that means rose bushes and borders; here, it means a view of the wide river and a three-foot patch of grass that hasn't been chewed apart by fire ants."

"Show away." Maggie gave me a small, tight smile that took obvious effort. "But I'm not sure how English I actually am anymore. Too much travelling about. Too many years in New York. Neither fish nor fowl."

I groaned at the cliché. "You've been hanging around Bear too much."

We picked our way down the yard toward the riverbank. In the old days, all the houses on the river had sea walls, but now Seminole Beach has a law limiting their construction. Mine was grandfathered in, and I plopped down gratefully on top of it, dangling my feet over the side.

After a minute or so, Maggie did the same.

It was dark except for lights from houses across the water and still brighter ones that reflected off the big bridge around the bend. A white foamy tide was *whooshing* in, making rapid inroads on the miniature beach below our feet. The smooth crescent of sand had about three minutes before being wiped out.

"What's going on with Bear, then?" Maggie managed.

"How do you mean?"

She pushed her red hair behind her ears with both hands. "The surfing lesson, searching my room, taking a bottle of vodka when he thought I wasn't looking,." She pulled in a rasping breath. "What's he supposed to be? My keeper?"

I sat up, straightening both my spine and resolve. "I'm glad you brought that up. Here's the deal. I've known Bear several years, and he's a little quirky, but I trust him as much as I do you, and you can't go on like this. Depression can kill you. I know that from personal experience. So," I took a breath and plunged on, "I asked him to boot camp you for a week, which means a lot of stuff you probably don't want to do. Bear runs every morning, and you'll have to run too. And he'll make you eat a lot of stuff you don't like."

"Christ, Keegan!" Maggie snapped at me, almost animated, "You've got balls!"

"I know. But the alternative is, you go back to New York and deal with it there. It's up to you. Bear thinks it's a lot of effort, but he's willing to give it a try. You think you can take off work for a week or so?"

She looked away, but not before I saw tears start in her eyes again.

"Sure. Why not? I, um, don't actually have a job there anyway."

"But Amy met you at . . ."

"I had one then. My editor got fed up with my absences — the times I had to rescue Stubb from whatever trouble he'd got into. She gave me one of those providential last chances and told me to choose the job or him." She forced a laugh.

"God, Maggie. You should have said something."

Her shoulders hunched up around her ears. "What am I going to do? No job, my reason for losing the job gone . . ." She stopped and looked down the river, head down, tears falling onto her lap.

I reached out and rubbed her shoulder. "For now, you stay here. For the next week, you just do whatever Bear tells you and see how it goes."

She didn't say anything, and I figured it was fifty-fifty. The old Maggie would have agreed she had nothing to lose. This one had been genetically altered by death and booze and who knew what else.

The river was even darker by the time we went in the house, lights still shimmering off the dense black water. As Maggie went off to bed, I started up to the mezzanine and met Kenji on the stairs. He looked unsettled.

"Keegan. Have you . . . did you take away prints of . . . the three men?"

"The guys on the picnic table? No, why?"

Kenji's English got even more distorted, and his eyes were troubled. "Because when they are . . . back in my room, two . . . missing from the pile."

Chapter 12

Kenji's two missing photographs were still missing the next morning, although he and I turned the kitchen upside down and searched the hall and stairway. Nobody else had seen them either.

I waited until Bear was out running with Maggie before I drove to Lost River. I hadn't forgotten my promise to Bear that we'd investigate together, but I wanted to track down the bartender I'd seen at the Whole Hog Saloon by myself. Women will tell you the truth faster when there isn't a good-looking guy hanging in the background, and Bear doesn't do background very well. Also, I wanted to take another shot at finding the girl Stubb had supposedly seduced, the one who routinely cleaned the church.

Lee Lee was with me, riding shotgun, again bound for St. Jude's miracle earth room.

"You've been at the church every day this week," I said. I passed a truckload of sod and sped along the canal. "Aren't you tired of it?"

"Oh, no, I get such a — hopeful feeling when I'm there. Just being in the same room with all that incredible energy."

"But that takes ten minutes, max. What do you do the rest of the time?"

She looked sideways at me, startled. "Why, just sit in the church. Waiting for . . . um, messages."

"What kind of messages?"

She thought for a moment. "Mostly, that quiet little voice that tells me what I'm supposed to do next. I used to hurt myself just walking through this life. I had to learn to get past the world's noise — just to listen. I learned that in Peru — on the Island of the Moon. It's really remote there and they have magic rocks."

"Really?" *Magic rocks?*

She nodded her head, blonde ponytail flopping. "It's where divine feminine energy is stored on the planet. And we went up on the mountain and meditated for hours. It was really dark, and there we were, all alone, out in the middle of nowhere."

"Is Peru that safe?"

"Probably not." She sighed. "But the shaman was with us."

"The shaman?"

"Our spiritual guide. But he didn't go up the mountain, he waited on the boat. Only he got into the ceremonial wine, and when we got back, he threw his arms around me and breathed booze fumes in my face. It was a little embarrassing. I mean, how can you blow off a shaman?"

I didn't have an answer for that, but it didn't matter. Two seconds later, Lee Lee had shifted her attention to the rows of citrus trees running parallel with the road.

"Isn't it amazing?" she remarked, looking out the window. "Lost River is only a few miles from Seminole Beach, but it's like a whole different country. No beaches, no tourists, no traffic. But if this weird weather keeps up — global warming or whatever — if the Antarctic keeps melting and the sea level keeps rising, it'll mean a lot more than just beach erosion. I've seen those old maps of Florida. In older, prehistoric times, it was twice the size it is today. And you know what that means."

"No, what?"

"That in thirty or forty years, Lost River could be on the beach. Which means condos and motels and thousands of exhaust-spewing cars. It'll be totally ruined."

I looked over to see if she was kidding, but her face was absolutely serious.

Well, damn. I didn't care if Lost River's inhabitants swapped their old-Florida ambience for waterfront, and they probably didn't either, but I did care if my house was covered in ocean. Particularly during my lifetime. Never mind saving the earth, in the Sunshine State it's all about real estate and short-term self-interest.

I dropped Lee Lee at St. Jude's, then drove down a couple of side streets until I found the Whole Hog Saloon. I wasn't counting on it being open in the daytime, and it wasn't, but I was hoping a cleaning crew might be there. God knows it needed one.

My hope was only partially realized. The back door was standing wide open, and a woman was stacking black plastic bags around several dented garbage cans. She was bent over, coffee colored and too old to be doing that kind of work.

"Hi," I said, as she straightened up and saw me approach. "Sorry to bother you, but I'm looking for the bartender who works here. Long hair, cowboy boots."

The woman cocked her head at me. "They all got long hair and boots."

"Really? How many women work here?"

"Don't know."

"Okay. This one is young with dark brown hair."

The woman turned to go back inside. "One of 'em works days over to the Circle K," she said and shut the door.

I drove back out to the main drag and found the Circle K, but the woman at the counter was forty years too old to be the girl I was seeking. However, the one hauling in boxes of spring water from the back room was the one who'd waited on me the night I rescued Stubb.

Not that she was easy to recognize. For this job, she twisted her long dark hair into a knot at the back of her head and wore shapeless clothes. She frowned when she saw me walking in her direction, and I realized she was older than I'd guessed by maybe ten years.

I got a Diet Coke out of the wall cooler and pretended to be surprised. "Hey, you were in the bar the other night. Which reminds me, you know those guys sitting at the table? One of them was lying face down. Somebody called him Porky Joe."

The girl was still frowning. "Yeah? What about them?"

"They were in St. Jude's churchyard the next night," I began, but she pushed her bottom lip out and interrupted me.

"I don't know who they were; guys are in and out all night long. And lots of people sit in the churchyard after dark. They're not supposed to drink in public, but nobody says anything. Not unless they cause some kind of trouble."

"Maybe I'll drop in at the Whole Hog one night this week. Maybe they'll be there then."

"Could be, no idea." Her eyes narrowed. "You're doing something for Ms. Butler, right?"

I expect the surprise showed on my face. "Does everybody in this town know everybody else's business?"

"Pretty much. But you wanna be careful with her. Comes out on top of whatever situation she gets in, and the people she's dealing with don't usually. Money and getting even are what gets her out of bed mornings."

"You have some particular situation in mind? Something you know about personally?"

"Personally?" The girl's laugh was without humor. "No, I don't get in the way of what people want personally. Particularly when they've got a bad case of foremanitis."

"Excuse me?"

"Never mind." She turned her back on me, grasped a cardboard container and pulled a box cutter out of her pocket.

I stood there watching her. "I still don't understand why they call the guy Porky Joe."

She raised her head and stared at me. "You don't wanna know." Then she slashed the top off the box with one quick movement.

Definitely time to go. I went out and got in the BMW and drove to the street where the church-cleaning girl lived.

The girl's name was Elena, and this time she answered the door herself. She was pretty, dark haired and a little on the hefty side. I could hear somebody whispering in the background, but she ignored whoever it was.

"What do you want?"

"I came by yesterday to ask about Stubb Flanders, but you

weren't home. You know, the photographer? The one who had the — uh — accident at St. Jude's?"

"Oh, him." She didn't seem upset by his death. "He is not so great. He only cares about fingermarks and cleaning. I tell him, you touch things, they get dirty. You touch every day, they get very dirty. But he makes me clean and watches to see I do it."

"You mean the front doors?"

She looked bored enough to expire on the spot. "No, the door on the side. Also the walls. And the little window in the back room."

"Did he say why?"

"No. After that, we have other things to talk about. My father was very mad, but I said he paid me extra to clean those things, so who cares." She gave me a sidelong glance. "You pay me to talk to you now?"

"Well, no, I just wanted —"

Wrong answer. The door closed in my face and didn't open when I knocked on it again.

I went back to St. Jude's to pick up Lee Lee, and drove home.

Bear was in the kitchen, trying to get Maggie to drink a blender full of something green and frothy. She kept making gagging sounds, and he finally told her to hold her nose and swallow. Afterward, she went upstairs to lie down.

"She sleeps too much," he said to me. "Needs something to keep her mind occupied. Amy's at the grocery store. Where've you been?"

I told him about Elena, the cleaning girl and my conversation with the Whole Hog bartender. "What do you think foremanitis is?"

He laughed at me. "Same thing you do. Since you decided to investigate on your own, maybe I'll do the same. We can't both go tonight anyway; somebody has to keep tabs on Maggie."

"Fine with me. I'm already tired of the commute."

Chapter 13

When he headed out around ten that night, Bear was wearing worn-thin jeans, sneakers and a T-shirt that read: I can't go to work today. The voices said, *Stay home and clean the guns.*

"Is it Halloween?" I remarked, when he came into the kitchen.

He gave me a disgusted look. "You don't talk to cowboys and farmers in khakis and a golf shirt. Look like some damn preppie."

Lee Lee, who'd been hanging around downstairs, offered to ride out to Lost River with him, but after a level look from Amy, she suddenly remembered the church closed at six thirty and disappeared in the direction of her room. I went upstairs, set my alarm for a four a.m. Maggie-check and went to bed.

I'm not sure what time Bear got home, but he was downstairs before noon the next day, soaking up coffee and telling anybody who'd listen about his Whole Hog experience.

It was a typical Bear presentation and he was full of himself, but he'd done much better than I had by just sitting at the bar listening to locals. The girl bartender on duty — not the one with the box cutter — had turned out to be the mother lode when it came to gossip. She was also best buddies with the girl I'd tracked down at Circle K. Bear got not only the names of the three guys we were looking for, but also the address of a woman who supposedly lived with one of them. And as a bonus, he had the scoop on Candy Butler.

"The word is Candy Butler takes no prisoners," Bear reported with a smile, clearly pleased with himself. "She's pissed off a lot of people over the years and keeps her foreman on a short leash. Which doesn't make your Circle K girl happy. She and Pete were apparently having a thing, and Ms. B warned her off. Threatened her, according to my sources," he said, looking smug. "But, more important than that, Candy Butler has a legitimate reason for thinking the police will go after her over Stubb's killing."

I put down my coffee cup. "And that would be?"

"She shot her husband dead about twenty-two years ago."

"You're kidding? And didn't go to jail? Or did she?"

"Didn't." Bear answered. "Claimed it was an accident. A neighbor's dog got loose and was chasing the horses, and she fired at it with a rifle. She shot twice and hit the dog once. The other bullet got her husband in the chest."

"Funny, she didn't mention it when she invited me to lunch." I sat back in my chair and thought for a minute. "Well, if you're not exhausted from your night on the town, we may as well drive out there again this afternoon. I'll talk Amy into watching Maggie for a couple of hours."

"We gonna look for Porky Joe and his buddies?"

I nodded. "You've got their address, and we better check it out while it's still good. I want to know exactly what those guys saw the night Stubb died before I have any more talks with Candy Butler."

We found the address we were looking for in a weedy, decrepit trailer park a mile out of Lost River. Most of the trailers looked uninhabitable, but I had a feeling they weren't. The woman who supposedly cohabited with one of the three farm workers lived in a rusty beige number with plywood nailed over the windows, straight into the metal siding. It sat on concrete blocks, and the front door stood open with only a single, broken, cement block for a step.

Bear planted himself on the partial block and pounded on the outside of the trailer wall.

"Hey, Joe here? Anybody home?"

No sound came from inside. He waited a couple of seconds and pounded louder.

After another, longer wait, somebody, or something, began to move around inside, and eventually, a voice grunted out a question.

Bear took it as an invitation and stepped up through the open door, motioning for me to follow.

The room we entered was part kitchen, part living room. Flies buzzed around a tottery card table covered with food: a loaf of soft, white bread, open jars of honey and mayonnaise, and packages of ripped-apart bologna, already turning brown and yellow. A very large cockroach clung to the table leg, its feelers darting around before it dropped to the floor. A diaper — clearly used — was under the table.

On the living room side, a single, stained piece of sectional couch, a portable TV and a glass topped coffee table were crammed together. The glass top was broken in two large pieces, one of which lay on the floor. The sour smell of filth and something like onions was so strong, I kept turning my nose back to the open doorway for air.

A man was standing in the tiny hallway looking at us. He wore khaki shorts and a yellow T-shirt, and his hands were shaking. A partly dried, red-brown stain had soaked through the front of the yellow shirt and dripped onto his shorts. He was barefooted and hadn't shaved for at least a week.

"You the guy they call Porky Joe?" Bear said, staring at him.

The man brushed long, dark brown hair out of his eyes, saw me standing behind Bear and visibly flinched. "What? No. No, I'm not. I'm Red."

"Don't mind the lady," Bear said to him. "She's not HRS or anything. You might have seen her at St. Judes's church a couple nights ago."

"Hell, you police?" Red's voice was jittery. "They've already been here asking questions. I told them, and I'll tell you — we go there sometimes. Sit and drink. Don't bother anybody. No big deal."

Bear looked at me, and I shrugged. Red could have been one of the guys on the picnic table, but he wasn't one of the two I'd seen at the Whole Hog. Unless he was the face down one.

Bear waved a dismissive hand. "We're not police. Just a few questions about the night Stubb Flanders died. You know, the guy in the dirt room."

Red tried to shove his hands into his pockets to keep from

shaking, but he missed, and they ended up clinging to his thighs. "I — I — I don't . . ." His whole body began to shudder as if his insides were being torn out.

I couldn't stand it; it brought back too many memories of my ex-husband. I grabbed a grubby spoon off the kitchen table and wiped it on my shirt. Then I scooped a spoonful out of the open jar of honey and shoved it in his mouth.

He was past surprise, just opened his eyes wider and spent a couple of seconds trying to swallow it. When he did, I gave him another shot of the honey and turned to Bear.

"The alcoholic's two-second cure. My area of expertise. He needs to sit down."

Red obediently edged backward onto the odd piece of couch. It took a couple of minutes, but eventually his hands shook quite a lot less and he got a whole sentence out.

"I could use a drink." His voice was weak. "Just a little one. I fell awhile ago." His hand indicated the broken glass on the floor. "The table cut me." He raised up his T-shirt to reveal a wide gash that ran from just under his right nipple to his left side. It was still oozing blood.

"You're gonna need stitches for that," Bear told him.

"I need a drink," Red repeated.

"Hold on a minute." Bear looked down at him. "You got to the church the night Stubb Flanders died around nine o'clock, and you stayed 'til after one o'clock the next morning. You sat facing the side door the whole time. You see anybody go near it while you were there?"

The man shook his head no and crossed his arms around his stomach. "We, uh, I was, uh, tryin' not to have a drink, but there was . . . a bottle." He looked down at his shirt and weakly brushed at the blood stains.

"Who were you drinking with?"

The man hesitated, then said, "Carlo and, um, Joe."

Bear stared at him. "Do they live here? In the trailer?"

"Not really, sometimes, when they can't make it home. You guys aren't cops?"

Bear acted as if he hadn't heard. "Who else lives here?"

"Uh, Joe's girlfriend. She's got a baby." He looked around the room as if just realizing he was the only one there. "It's her place. She's working, I guess. Musta took the kid with her."

"So Joe does live here?"

The guy shrugged. "Sometimes. Sometimes it's just her and me and Mayo."

"Mayo?"

Red's tanned face flushed with embarrassment. "Her kid. They call him that. He was okay 'til he was about two. Somebody hit him in the head with a mayonnaise jar."

"You?"

"Christ, no. I wasn't even around then."

"Where are your two friends today? Working?"

"Yeah. Finishing the sweet onions."

"How do you get to the onion field?"

The man looked upset again. "You can't go over there; you'll get 'em fired. Come back tonight. They'll be here tonight."

Red refused to accept a ride to get stitched up, so I talked Bear into driving me out to the Butler Ranch. I had decided to go ahead and ask Candy why she hadn't mentioned shooting her husband. But Ms. Butler was out for the evening. Since her Jeep was sitting in front of a double garage and a sedan was in the other berth, it occurred to me that Candy was avoiding me, but the cook said she had flown to Vero Beach for dinner in her Piper Cub and wouldn't be back until late. I wanted to ask if the foreman had gone with her but decided that was too pushy.

Bear and I had fried chicken at the Mikasuki Inn while we waited for the onion diggers to finish work. I called Amy to make sure Maggie was okay, and she said not to worry, they were making ciabatta bread. Poor Maggie. That was another thing she'd never wanted to do: cook.

On our way back to the trailer, Bear stopped and picked up a small bottle of bourbon. I think he felt sorry for Red and was buying him a drink against his better judgment, but Red wasn't there, and nobody seemed to know where he'd gone.

Red's two friends, Joe and Carlo, had apparently arrived just before us, and they needed a bath in the worst way. Carlo had dark skin and eyes and a mustache, and Joe had rusty, almost orange hair. A heavy-hipped, dark-haired woman was frying something on the stove. The odor of blackened hotdogs only partially edged out the smell of sweat and dirt. The used diaper was still on the floor.

Bear put the bottle of bourbon on the table, and both men looked instantly happy. They poured themselves drinks in stained plastic juice cups and offered me one, which I refused. Bear held onto his while he talked but didn't taste it.

The men were friendly enough and, unlike Red, didn't seem to care who we were or why we were there. The girl look resigned, like it wasn't the first time and wouldn't be the last time total strangers had invaded her living space with peremptory questions. She never spoke while we were there, and there was no sign of a mayonnaise-jar-damaged two year old.

"We didn't see nobody," Joe told Bear in response to his questions about the church. "We was talking and having a drink, but nobody come around. Oh, some girl went around back and said something to a guy in a chair, but she didn't stick around."

That would have been Lee Lee.

"Nobody else?" I put in. "How about an older woman with black hair? Did you see her talking to the guy in the chair?"

"No." Joe took a slug of bourbon. "Didn't see the guy after awhile. Looked up once and the chair was there but not him."

"Do you remember what time that was?"

"Not really. Hour or so after we got there, maybe. Lot of people walking out front, but nobody come in the yard."

"And you didn't see anybody go near the side door?" Bear grilled him.

"Nope." He scratched the back of his head. "We talked it over after we found out what happened to that guy. Carlo didn't see nobody . . ." He paused and waited until Carlo nodded agreement, "and I didn't, and old Red was awake the whole time, and he didn't." A big smile split his face. "Pretty much covers it."

"But you didn't go tell the police?"

Joe looked at him incredulously. "Hey, I don't crap in my own sleeping bag."

Bear glanced over at the dark-haired man and repeated, "Didn't see anybody at all the whole night?"

Carlo's head went slowly back and forth. "Solamente mis amigos," he said with a smirk.

Joe scratched at his orange head and shrugged.

Chapter 14

The garage guy called just after nine o'clock the next morning to say my back window had come in and they could install it any time. I was tired of driving around town in a wind tunnel, so I hustled down before they got busy.

My garage is small, family owned, and Sinatra songs blast out of the back room, nonstop. The mechanics are all hot-looking Italian guys with tight biceps and other interesting parts. Ordinarily, I would have stuck around just to soak up the ambience while they toiled away, but this time I walked four blocks to the library to do a little research. My computer at home died long ago, so I log onto one of our tax supported ones if I need to look up anything serious. Otherwise, I rely on my cell phone or I ask Kenji.

There was nothing on Candy Butler, not under her previously

married name, or Butler, or Butler Horse Farms. Even when I tried "Shooting Deaths in 1980's Florida," it was awhile before I found anything, and that was curious too. Newspaper clippings that had originally covered the case were unavailable for viewing. I kept getting that empty, annoying page that said the site was being updated.

The court case was a matter of record, but it only rated one paragraph on a docket with several others. Apparently, Ms. Butler had testified, the grand jury found no reason to further investigate, and the state's forensic evidence was not incompatible with her version of the incident. Three snappy sentences, and that was it. No other information about the shooting, not even the name of her dead husband.

Bear had written down the last names of Joe, Carlo and Red, as supplied by his Whole Hog bartender friend, but there was no record of any of them on the internet. The names were probably all bogus anyway. I gave up the search after I Googled Bobby McCleod and found less information than I already had.

By the time I drove my newly repaired vehicle home, the house was deserted. Amy had left a note saying she was at the vegetable market, Kenji's door was locked, Jesse wasn't on the sun porch, and Bear, Maggie and Lee Lee were nowhere to be found.

There was a time when I'd have reveled in the silence of an empty house, but today I had too much nervous energy. I got back in the car, drove out to the beach and walked all the way to the inlet and back. The wind blew my hair and restlessness all around, and the sand was warm on my feet. Seventy-eight gorgeous degrees and another day in paradise; the tourists had it right. Until global warming covered my house with a tidal wave. Maybe I should put it up for sale now, get ahead of the curve.

Amy's Jeep was parked out front when I returned. Some kind of sauce was simmering on the stove, so she wasn't far away, but the house was oddly still. I was on my way up to the mezzanine when I heard voices and assorted noises coming from the third floor and detoured to have a look.

Number Seven is the only uninhabited room on third. Bear has Number Nine, Kenji Number Six and Amy the much smaller Number Eight, but Seven has been empty since the naked hairdresser moved out, which is another story and one best forgotten. Anyway, about a year ago, somebody slapped a coat of thick, white paint on Seven, moved in a metal banquet table and stacked up an entire wall of old lockers, every size and shape. Everyone uses the room if they have a project or need extra space. Jesse spent a week there once carving clay flower petals, and Kenji stores photography equipment in the big lockers.

Today, the room looked like a command center for the military — if the military was on a restricted budget. Bear was hammering away on his manual typewriter at one end of the banquet table, Maggie was at the other end downloading and printing out information, and Kenji was taping a six-foot length of white shelf paper to one wall. Lost River was scrawled in six-inch letters across the top of the paper, and several photographs and bits of paper were already attached to its surface.

"What's going on?" I said to Bear as I scanned the taped notes: Small window in rear of church? Church roof intact, replaced in 2009? Check with priest?

His blue eyes were bright, but his voice was extremely offhand. "Just a little research. Never know when it'll come in handy." He motioned with his head toward the landing. "Come out for a minute."

Bear pulled the door shut behind us and lowered his voice. "It's really for Maggie. She needs something to do, so I made her my research assistant. She's a journalist; she can do investigative reporting. It'll keep her mind off her problems."

"You're kidding. She's going to research her own boyfriend's murder? And then what? You write a book about it?"

"C'mon, Keegan. It's not like that. Although it wouldn't be a bad story. Anyway," he paused long enough to signal a shift in subject, "has it occurred to you that Maggie makes as good a suspect as Ms. Butler?"

"Are you nuts? Maggie loved Stubb."

"Maybe so, but she wasn't in New York the night he died. She was here, in Florida."

"She was not. I talked to her. She missed her plane."

"This was in her suitcase." Bear handed me a credit card receipt from the Airways Motel in Palm Beach. "Check the date."

I did. Maggie Gilchrist had signed the motel receipt the same day Stubb was killed. My friend Maggie, the most honest person I could think of, had been lying like a rug with fringe.

I would have demanded an immediate explanation, but Bear thought Maggie was too fragile to be questioned, and if Bear considered her fragile, she was probably freaking falling apart. I was so bummed, I went back downstairs, got in my car and drove to the Dairy Queen.

Most of a chocolate dip-cone later, I decided to run the errand I'd put off a couple of days ago: check the library at Seminole Beach High for pictures of Candy Butler's twin boys. As Bobby McCleod's old eighth-grade teacher had reminded me, schools know everything. There should be teachers, advisors, old friends around who still remembered the boys and, by extension, their mother. Shifting into information-gathering mode might take my mind off Maggie.

It was after three when I got there, and everybody but the secretaries had gone home. Public school security measures are big news these days, and I was prepared to show my driver's license or be fingerprinted or wear one of those sticky ID tags. However, the woman at the administration desk merely pointed me down the sidewalk toward the media center, without inquiring who I was or why I had an overwhelming desire to see old yearbooks.

The library had ultra-tall ceilings, bright light coming in from high windows and banks of computers. It even had some books. A cheerful woman brought me yearbooks from 1982 through 1986, also without asking who I was or why I wanted them. So much for security. There was a screening device as I entered the main doors, but it was impossible to tell if it was to keep you from importing a weapon or making off with a few computers.

I flipped through page after page of class officers, soccer and wrestling meets, football, basketball, tennis, band, French club and swim team members before I found what I wanted in "Graduating Seniors of 1985." Scott and Bobby McCleod, mirror images in dark jackets, black bow ties and ruffled white shirts, were in row three. Except for the eyes, they looked exactly alike.

Scott's eyes held a daredevil glint. Bobby's were less confident and a little wistful, as if he'd lost something that couldn't be replaced. Scott had played football, Bobby soccer. Both had belonged to the Spanish club. Both listed photography and surfing as interests. They were such baby-faced, geeky-looking kids, I couldn't imagine them ever growing into self-supporting adults.

I continued to page through 1985, looking at snapshots of seniors hanging out at the beach or mugging on the school steps, but Candy's twins didn't run to candid shots.

The 1984 yearbook wasn't much better. Ms. Butler's boys managed to look even dorkier as juniors. I was just flipping to the faculty section when a shot of two boys on skateboards got my attention. After a minute, I realized they were only Scott-Bobby look-alikes, but the girl in the background, watching the boys do wheelies, seemed familiar. I squinted up my eyes, decided it couldn't be her, then decided it was. There were no cut lines for any of the candid shots, and the girl in the picture had dark hair, but that dizzy-breezy smile was either Lee Lee's or her twin sister's.

I searched for her class photo in the junior section and found it easily. In 1984, before she'd changed from brunette to platinum blonde, Luane Keiner had attended high school with the McCleod twins. However, she was nowhere to be found in the 1985 yearbook. Had she flunked out or gotten married or been adopted her last year of high school?

I was so taken back, I forgot about the teachers, advisors or old friends who might know Candy Butler; instead, I asked to use the copy machine, then drove home faster than I should have. I didn't know what the police were turning up, but every time I found a new piece of information involving Stubb's death, it pointed in the direction of my house.

Bear was still in Number Seven, hunched over his decrepit Royal typewriter like a plot-driven Hemingway. Periodically, he tossed a scrawled note to faithful sidekick Maggie, who searched websites to support his latest wild idea.

I hesitated in the doorway, reluctant to interrupt such an inspired performance, and Kenji came out of his room with a handful of photos.

"Ah, Keegan," he said, fanning them out. "Have replaced two missing pictures — of men on picnic tables. Also enlarged."

"Good, I've got some too." I showed him my Xerox copies of the McCleod twins' junior and senior photos. Then I handed him the picture of the skateboarders.

"See the girl in the background? She look familiar?"

Kenji's head nodded slowly. "Yes. Lee Lee?"

Bear, the only guy I know who can actually do two things at once, had been listening to our conversation while he typed. He got up and came around the table to look.

"It is her." He took the copy out of Kenji's hand and glanced at me. "This out of a yearbook?"

I nodded. "Nineteen eighty-four. She went to high school, right here in River City."

"No shit." His eyebrows rose almost to his hairline. "That's worth a question or two. Anybody seen her around lately?"

"Maybe her room." Kenji was still studying the picture.

"I'll find her." I turned and headed downstairs.

Lee Lee wasn't in her room or in the second floor bathroom or in the kitchen. She wasn't in any of the rooms downstairs either, but when I stepped out on the front porch, I heard her voice coming from Jesse's sunroom studio.

"Like this?" It was definitely her, and she sounded almost indecently mellow.

"Exactly like that," Jesse agreed, "support it at all times. It's dangerous to use just one hand. You have to become totally lost in it, that's the joy of it."

Oh, great. And with both of his doors standing open too. At least they were behind the white wicker screen Jesse used to divide his sleeping quarters from his pottery wheels. I began backing quietly away.

"Better now?" Jesse again.

"Mhhhh hmmm. Sometimes I just get so upset . . ."

"You'll be on top of the world in a minute. Let's just finish it off . . ."

Lee Lee giggled, and Jesse groaned. "There you go. That's it. Both hands now, support your clay at all times . . ."

I stopped backing up and went to look around the screen. Lee Lee was sitting at a small potting wheel with Jesse beside her, trying to keep a sodden mass of gray mud from flying off into the wall. They both looked happier than pigs in slop.

"You must allow others just to be. As long as you resist, they persist. Validate them and permit them to exist without your input." Jesse murmured

"Yes." It came out in a long, ecstatic sigh. If her voice echoed her mind, she was definitely in some altered state. Like Texas.

I interrupted. "Lee Lee, could I speak to you for a second?"

She jumped a little and turned to look at me. "Sure, what's up? Can you take this, Jesse?"

He replaced her hold on the clay with his own hands and slid onto her stool while she followed me out to the front porch.

Her white-blonde hair was down around her shoulders, and she frowned at her muddy hands as if she wasn't sure how they'd gotten that way.

"I thought you'd never been to Lost River before?" I said abruptly. Dealing with Candy Butler was having a detrimental effect on my manners. "You went to Seminole Beach High in the Eighties. How could you never have been to Lost River?"

She stopped frowning at her fingers and looked up. "I never said I hadn't been there, I said I'd never been to St. Jude's Church. We weren't Catholic, and anyway, they didn't have the healing earth when I lived here. My family moved to Miami long before that happened. That's one of the reasons I was so interested in coming up here — just to experience it. I didn't mean to mislead you."

Lee Lee's blue eyes were confused, verging on hurt, and I found myself apologizing before retreating back upstairs. If she was the same age as the McCleod twins, she'd moved away at least a dozen years before St. Jude's miracle.

Bear was waiting for me. "What'd she say?"

"Why?" I snapped at him. "Weren't you leaning over the banister, listening?"

"Yep." He gave me a big grin. "Opened the window over the porch too. But her voice doesn't carry."

I repeated Lee Lee's explanation, and he shrugged. "Well, it could be. You were sitting there with her all night. You didn't fall asleep and let her slip inside, did you?"

I shook my head.

"Then it doesn't matter. All that matters is how somebody got in the church. I think we're going to have to take a look. See if the stained glass windows are really wired. Check that weird little window in the back room. Let's do it."

"Now? It's four-thirty. Besides, with all the publicity, there's liable to be a line clear around the building."

Bear ignored my input. "I'll see if Amy needs the Jeep. If she does, we'll take your car."

"I'm not going."

"Sure you are." Bear glanced at Maggie, who was still staring at the computer, and made a face at me. "Maggie too."

I started to say that was probably a bad idea, but Maggie got in ahead of me.

"It's okay, I want to look at the dirt room. Now's as good a time as any." Her voice was flat and her eyes were back to staring again.

Terrific.

Chapter 15

Despite my misgivings, there were only eight people waiting in St. Jude's main aisle. We were the last to queue up, which suited Bear since it left him free to inspect the outside pews and stained glass windows without attracting too much attention.

The church was built like a T, with a long aisle down the center, an altar at the end and three rooms behind the altar forming the crossbar. The larger room to the right, once a storeroom, was now the sacristy, although the *Seminole Beach Sentinel* called it a dressing room. The two smaller rooms to the left had been labeled healing room and library in the same article. The place was built like a miniature fortress, but I saw Father Mike's point. It was too small to provide hiding places; anybody crouching in the pews would be spotted immediately.

The line kept moving forward, about a foot at a time, and eventually we reached the communion rail and took a left. At that point, Maggie shifted from motionless silence to such a case of jitters, I was afraid she'd have a fit. When it was our turn, I motioned her into the healing room and stepped back, away from the open door. If she intended to throw herself full length across the dirt, sobbing hysterically, I didn't want to watch.

While I waited, Bear and Kenji checked out the priest's dressing room and the tiny library. When they returned, they reported all three rooms devoid of anything interesting.

Fortunately, there was no sign of anybody official to ask what they were up to, which made me wonder. If whoever in charge wasn't in the sacristy or the main part of the church or the two small rooms, where are they? Who was keeping an eye on things?

Maggie stayed in the earth room a long time. When she came out, there were marks of tears on her face but no signs she'd been tearing out her hair. She said she was going to sit in the church and left me to the magic dirt.

I passed. I did glance through the open doorway on my way down the hall, but the circle of earth was so smooth, I couldn't even remember where Stubb's body had been. It was impossible to believe somebody had died violently here, let alone someone I knew.

The infamous alarm key pad was attached at eye level on the wall next to the side door. It had an old-fashioned look, although it was only supposed to be a dozen years old. The key pad itself, the wall and the back of the door smelled faintly of Pine Sol cleaner. Elena had apparently taken Stubb's criticism to heart.

I stepped outside, happy to be out of the fusty building. There were no onion pickers sitting at the picnic table today.

No mark in the grass where Stubb's chair had been three nights earlier. No lingering trace or feel of Stubb or his activities. It was like none of it had ever happened.

Bear and Kenji eventually came out the side door and joined me.

"I want to show you something everybody else in town knows about." Bear led us to the spot where Stubb had been sitting, then through the screen of trees behind it. We came out in an empty field — empty except for the huge pile of soft, dark earth in the middle of it.

"See that? Truck brings it in every month or so. And some of it gets hauled into the healing room nearly every day."

I studied the pile of dirt. "That's why he sat in that particular spot. It put him between the dirt and the side door. But . . . what a total waste of effort."

"You got it." Bear turned and led the way back through the trees. "Father Durkin never claimed the dirt replaced itself, just like he never claimed it was responsible for the miracles. But your wacko friend, Stubb, thought it was his ticket to the big time."

There was nothing else to see at the back of the church, except the small, high window. Bear studied it for a couple of minutes then walked slowly around to the front, eyes fixed on the tin roof.

Kenji and I tagged along.

"Roof's pretty new, no rust anywhere," Bear remarked, "but you *could* get in that way."

"Sure," I said, enthusiastically. "Just climb the big tree in back, leap twenty feet to the roof, pry up a thick piece of galvanized tin without making a sound and drop thirty feet to the church floor. Piece of cake."

Both of them ignored me.

"Maybe foundations," Kenji said, thoughtfully. "Burglars tunnel into places all . . . the time. Also hide in ducts of air conditioning."

I groaned. "You guys watch too much TV."

We had turned the corner as I spoke, and there was Maggie, standing on the front steps of St. Jude's, waiting for us. Her fists were shoved in her pockets and her chin was buried in her jacket collar. If she'd had some kind of mystical experience, she didn't mention it, not then or on the way home.

Bear, who sat in front with me, talked enough for everybody. Having ruled out entry from the roof, the foundations or the stained glass windows, he was pinning his hopes on the little back window.

"The frame was wired on the inside," he admitted, "but I noticed the wires weren't actually attached to the circuit contact. Maybe they bypassed the connection for that window because it's small and high."

"Or because painted shut," Kenji put in.

"It *looked* painted shut," Bear agreed, "but Stubb could have pried it open and squeezed through. And then somebody followed him in, killed him and simply superglued it shut on the way out."

"Superglue, of course," I said helpfully, "I always carry a little around, myself, just in case. But wouldn't you see little flakes of dried paint or peeled spots from where Stubb pried it open?"

"No," Bear's voice was impatient, "Stubb had the girl, Elena, clean them away. Then he had her clean the door and the wall for . . ."

"Camouflage." Kenji said the word with pride. "Must talk to cleaning girl."

"Certainly," Bear said, "but first, we test the glue theory."

Dinner was ready when we got home: salmon filets Amy had baked in rock salt with dill and shallot butter, mashed potatoes with goat cheese, and pan roasted brussels sprouts. I ate too much of everything and washed it down with too much white burgundy then took my share of the bread pudding with bourbon sauce. The result was another night of twisted dreams. The worst one had strangers hiding in the walls of the house, and when they peeked out periodically, each had the evil, grinning face of Stubb Flanders. At three, I woke up in a cold sweat, stayed still long enough to realize I wasn't going back to sleep, and went down to the kitchen to see if there was any bread pudding left. *Yeah, yeah, I know.*

I never got as far as the refrigerator, however, because I saw light coming from the great room the minute I opened the stairway door.

When I went to look, Maggie was stretched out on the sofa watching *Ancient Aliens* on the old TV. Something dark and shiny was clutched to her chest and an empty wine bottle sat on the floor.

She rolled her head on the cushion and stared up at me. "Couldn't sleep."

"What are you holding?"

She hesitated, then lifted a Ziploc bag. "Some, uh, dirt from that room."

"Oh. Any wine left?"

She shook her head. "Drank it all. Sorry, Keegan. I know it isn't part of the program, but I couldn't help it." She squeezed the bag. "Stubb was laying right on it, Keegan. This dirt. I tried to sleep, but I couldn't."

"Why didn't you wake up Bear?"

"I was going to, but when I went to knock on his door . . .

he wasn't alone . . . Amy . . . I didn't want to interrupt."

"No." I sat down at the end of the couch, and she pulled her feet up to make room.

"It's my fault, you know." The wine had apparently punched her chatter button. "I made Stubb take this assignment. Pressured him. I thought it was good that he was actually interested in something, even if it was dirt. And it turns out to be the one place in the country where somebody wanted him dead — Bobby McCleod's home town. What kind of shitty coincidence is that?"

"Are you talking about Candy Butler?"

"Who else? "Her voice was bitter. "She blamed him for the death of her son. And according to you, for the drunk the other one became."

I studied her face. "Why didn't you tell me you were in Florida the night Stubb died? You didn't miss your plane; you stayed at a motel in West Palm."

Maggie shrugged. "Humiliated, I guess. Again. I actually got in around eight thirty that night."

"Why didn't you come to the house?"

"Because Stubb was in Lost River. My mobile started ringing two minutes after the plane landed. He was calling from behind the church, waiting for his big moment, and he couldn't wait to tell me. He was beyond hyped. He was going to get pictures of the priest salting the earth room with fake dirt and 'expose the whole phony enterprise'.

"As soon as I got the rental car, I made them give me a map and directions to Lost River. I tried calling him back, but he must have turned his phone off. And then, like the city girl I am, I got lost. Lost on the way to Lost River." Her laugh was brittle.

"All those turning, twisting roads, and it was horribly dark.

I went probably twenty miles in the wrong direction before I found a petrol station and got turned round. At ten fifteen, I was still miles away. That's when Stubb called me and said he was 'going in.' "

"Ten fifteen? Did he say how he'd get inside with the alarm on?"

Maggie shook her head. "He said St. Jude's was the biggest security joke in the world and he owed it all to an idiot priest and a cleaning girl. He told me he'd be inside before I got there but to park the car a couple of blocks away and come 'round back, through an empty field, so no-one would see me. Then he'd come get me and I could wait with him in the room for the 'moment of truth.' "

"Did he come?"

"No. I missed St. Jude's the first time through. Then I backtracked and parked and stumbled through some trees and waist-high weeds to the back of the church. Stubb's chair was there, and I waited, but he didn't come, and I knew he was going to mess it all up. There were some guys at a table on one side of the church, so I went to the opposite side and put Stubb's stool up to each of the windows to see if it would open. After a bit I found one that did, and I pushed it up."

"You actually opened one of the stained glass windows?"

She nodded. "It wasn't locked, but it only went up a few inches, not enough to squeeze through. So I called to him in a loud whisper."

She stared down at the bag of dirt, her voice uncertain. "He didn't answer, and I kept calling, and suddenly it all just washed over me. That was the norm the whole time I knew him: me calling out and Stubb not being there. I shut the window, returned the stool and went back the way I'd come — scratched hell out of myself on something large and spiky. By the time I got to the car, my arms and legs were all over blood."

She looked at me with a half smile. "Ironical, isn't it? The one time I summon enough nerve to leave, and he actually needed me. I turned off my mobile so he couldn't reach me and drove to West Palm. Just kept going until I saw the turn for the airport. But there weren't any flights until morning, so I stopped at an all-night pharmacy and got some antiseptic and a bottle of vodka and checked into a motel. I showered and put some stuff on my scratches, and then I had a drink. Several drinks."

She drew in a deep breath and held it for a moment.

"When I woke up it was noon, and I felt like dying," she continued. "I had a little more vodka — hair of the dog — and headed up this way. By that time, I decided Stubb just hadn't heard me calling, and I was going to walk in your house and let him wonder why I hadn't turned up the night before. And then, just as I left the interstate, I put on the radio . . . and I heard. I kept driving here. I didn't know what else to do."

Maggie's face was shiny with tears. I patted the foot that was lying closest to me.

After awhile I said, "Did Stubb explain why St. Jude's was 'the biggest security joke in the world'? Or what the cleaning girl said that gave him that idea?"

"No, but a lot of what he said made no sense. Like, the priest wouldn't give him any trouble about being in the dirt room because he wouldn't want to be 'banned in Boston.' Are you going to tell Bear that I was down here drinking? You are, aren't you?"

"Nope. You can do it when he takes you running tomorrow. Tell him the whole thing. Driving to Lost River the night Stubb died, drinking wine, the works. Bear's pretty good about some things. And he wants to help, Maggie."

She nodded slowly and even more slowly swung her feet around to the floor.

"You see why it was my fault? If I'd stayed at the church, not stomped off, Stubb would still be alive. He was all alone in there . . ." Her voice broke and she struggled to her feet and went out into the hall, clutching the Ziploc bag as if it were something precious.

I took the empty wine bottle to the kitchen and dropped it in the recycle bin, but my mind was fixed on church windows. If Maggie actually opened one of them, and no alarm went off, had it been immobilized, or was it never on in the first place? Was that Stubb's "biggest joke in the world"? Or was it that Father Mike never actually set the alarm, just let people think he did? And what the hell had the priest been up to in Boston?

It wasn't until I was back in my own bed that I considered Maggie's remark about being scratched up and bleeding in the churchyard. It made me wonder, How bloody would she be after whacking somebody with a camera tripod?

Chapter 16

Number Seven, now referred to by Bear as "the incident room," was fairly buzzing with activity the next morning. Maggie, having run two mandatory miles, was dutifully sipping a nasty-looking green drink when I walked in. Her red hair was combed, her eyes were red-rimmed but reasonably clear, and she seemed engrossed in her computer screen.

I walked behind her and saw she had keyed in "Father Mike Durkin" and "Boston," so I was pretty sure she had dumped the story of her nighttime transgressions on Bear.

Bear was hunched over his typewriter, and Kenji was posting notes on the wall of shelf paper with tiny slivers of scotch tape. Hours earlier, the two of them had glued one of Amy's kitchen windows shut before she came down stairs. After twenty minutes, they couldn't get it open without using a crowbar and had cracked two of the old panes in the process. Amy was not speaking to either of them.

One of Kenji's postings was from the *Jacksonville News* archives: a detailed account of the shooting of Candy Butler's husband.

I didn't bother asking how he'd managed to get it when I couldn't. Kenji knows how to do everything, including using Google's advance search function and a few other odd things for which he has a separate computer.

The clipping, dated 1980, was straightforward to the point of terse. Deputies had been called to the Butler Ranch by the foreman, Pete Beck. They found Gil Butler in a slough, dead from a gunshot to the chest. They also found the body of a dog nearby. Ms. Butler reported that the dog had been chasing her horses, and she'd gone out to run it off. She'd fired twice; the first shot missed, the second hit the dog. Afterward, she said she'd discovered her husband in a nearby ditch, dying from a wound in the chest. The article said the sheriff's department was investigating the incident.

I looked at the date again. Thirty-plus years ago. Interesting that Pete Beck had been working for Ms. Butler clear back then. Pete must be older than he looked.

Along with the clippings, Kenji had tacked up my yearbook copies of Scott and Bobby McCleod, both junior and senior versions. Also the one of Lee Lee watching the skateboarders. He was now attaching the enlargements he'd made of the three field-workers at the picnic table. He'd done a good job; even with the poor lighting, I could see Carlos' thick, black hair and moustache. Porky Joe's reddish-orange frizz nearly matched his red-tinted eyes. Just like the guy at the Whole Hog that night. And Red had the same lost, bewildered eyes I'd noticed at the trailer.

If the photos had been in black and white, I might have missed it. As it was, I felt like I'd been smacked in the back of the head by a large, impatient hand.

"Oh, shit."

Bear turned and stared at me. "What's wrong?"

"Us is what's wrong," I said, ungrammatically, "the stupidest, most —"

"What the hell are you talking about?"

"You and me. Look at them. We saw all three of them. Why would a guy with bright-red hair be called Joe and his dark-haired friend be tagged Red?"

"Are you making one of those famous intuitive leaps?" Bear said in a dubious voice. Then, "If you're right, he was smarter — even hungover — than we gave him credit for."

"What is it? What're you talking about?" Maggie left her chair and came to stand beside me.

"The guy who told Bear and me he was Red, wasn't. He was the one they call Porky Joe, but he gave Red's name. Maybe somebody told him we were looking for him — like the bartender who moonlighted at Circle K. Or maybe he and his roomies juggle names around all the time in case social services comes calling. Whatever it was, he gave Red's name then ran off to tell his friends so they could back him up." I shook my head. "I can't believe it. I actually saw Red and Carlos at the Whole Hog the night I went to find Stubb. Porky Joe must have been the one face down on the table. I would never have forgotten those eyes . . ."

I stopped talking and looked closer at the enlargement of Joe's face, then raised my head a couple of inches to take in the McCleod brothers' graduation head shots.

"Kenji," I murmured, almost to myself, "Do you think you can find more pictures of these boys somewhere? Something in color that clearly shows their faces about the time Scott was killed in Bolivia?"

Bear had moved closer to me. His eyes moved from the senior pictures to the guys on the picnic bench, then back again. "Not a chance, that's too much of a stretch."

"I know, but if you take away the long hair and add ten years or so . . . That's why I want something more current. I don't want to be fooled a second time."

I reached in my jeans pocket and pulled out my cell. Candy Butler answered her phone after six rings.

"It's Keegan Shaw," I told her. "We need to talk."

"Okay." I could hear her breathing hard over the connection. Maybe she was out jogging around the ranch. Maybe she was shooting her foreman in a ditch. That's the problem with cell phones; you never really know where anybody is.

She hesitated. "You want to talk now or not over the phone?"

"Not."

"Anything in particular?"

"Yes, I think I've found Bobby. At least I'm pretty sure I know where he was yesterday."

Silence, then, "You're not serious."

"Yeah, I am. I realize that wasn't the plan, but I think it's him. Also, I have some questions about your former husband."

Ms. Butler snorted. "I knew that was coming. Come out to the ranch around three o'clock. I'll be home by then, and you can hear the whole sad story." She hung up.

Bear was giving me the dubious face again. "Don't you

think you're jumping the gun? What if you find out it isn't Bobby?"

"I'm not wrong. It's him." I looked at the shelf paper pictures again. "Probably."

At two forty that afternoon, I was back on the road to Lost River. The sky was a clear blue, and the clouds were fluffy, heaped-up blobs of shaving cream, backlit by faded pink. If you paint clouds that way, they look fake.

Kenji had downloaded color pictures of the McCleod twins without any trouble. One, at age twenty-six, came from an old issue of *World Hot Spots*. The other two, at age twenty-eight, were from back issues of the *New York Times* Sunday supplement. They were very good, clear pictures, with all the geek from their high school years completely gone.

I compared the *Times* picture of Bobby McCleod with those of Porky Joe on the picnic bench and decided it was the same guy. True, he'd dropped twenty pounds over the years and his face had more sag and wrinkle than it should have had, but I was betting on those haunted eyes. I got Kenji to make copies of everything and shoved them in a manila folder, which now rested in the passenger seat. It would take his mother's identification to make sure.

I had expected Ms. Butler to be pleased when I turned up with news of her son's whereabouts; instead, I got a yawning, almost surly woman, who had done little to her face and hair before answering the front door.

"Sorry," she said in a tone that meant she wasn't really, "I've been up most of the night looking for a mare and a foal. Pete thinks somebody stole them right out of the damned stable."

"You don't think so?"

She grunted and led the way to a room in the back of the house. "Well, if they did, they're riding the mare bareback. Didn't take a saddle or bridle."

I hadn't seen her office the day I came to lunch. Except for the ornately framed pictures of horses that covered every wall, it was old-style and workmanlike: a bank of filing cabinets, and shelves of books on draft horses, equine breeding, foaling, artificial insemination and genetics. A plain, scarred, walnut desk was positioned in front of windows that overlooked the paddock area.

Ms. Butler's attitude didn't improve when I showed her the pictures. She dismissed the yearbook copies and newspaper clippings with a yawn. But she scowled for quite a long time at the enlarged photographs of Porky Joe and his friends in the churchyard.

"Could be, I guess," she said at last, "but I'd have to see him face to face. It's been five, six years." She tapped a finger on the photo. "You say this was taken the night Flanders died?"

I nodded. "Didn't you notice them on the north side of the church that night? Three guys at a picnic table drinking?"

"No, but I didn't go that way. I was being clever, sneaking up on Flanders." She closed the folder and pushed her chair back from the desk. "So, where is this guy now?"

"Living in a trailer on the other side of town. Picking onions." I handed her a slip of paper with the address.

Ms. Butler closed her eyes for a second, then opened them and got to her feet. "Sweet Jesus, he was here all the time? I better head over there and take a look. You want to come?"

"Sure. But I'd like to hear about your husband first. Why didn't you tell me about the shooting?"

"Former husband." She scowled, sat back down and pushed

both hands through her black curly hair. "I should have, I guess, but it's the kind of thing you hope will just go away and hardly ever does. It's also the kind of thing sheriff's deputies jump all over, so I got worried." She stared moodily at my manila folder, still on the desk in front of her. "I was hoping my past didn't get mixed up with the current problem."

When I didn't say anything, she sucked in a long, resigned breath. "It was a long time ago, and a lot of people have forgotten it. The neighbor down the road had a dog that liked to get over the fence and chase the horses. One day I'd had enough, and I got the rifle and hunted it down. My husband was out fixing fence in a ditch, and I never even saw him. The dog ran into where he was, and I shot.

"The sheriff," her voice was edged with scorn, "decided it was a suspicious death and made life hell for about four months before the grand jury said it was an accident. I never forgave that asshole for what he did to my boys. They were devastated. Had to take them out of school and send them to a relative. When he ran for sheriff the second time, I made sure the bastard didn't have a chance."

Her cell phone went off without warning and she picked it up off the desk. I could hear the foreman's voice as if he were in the room. Ms. Butler turned to me and repeated the message anyway.

"Guy rounding up calves spotted a foal down out by the oak hammock. Hurt, he thinks." She turned back to the phone, "Bring up my horse, will you, Pete? And saddle one for Keegan, okay? We've still got talking to do."

She turned to me. "You can ride, can't you?" Her voice was tired and impatient, and I wasn't about to admit most of my riding experience involved a Shetland pony named Shorty Bug.

"Uh, sure." I said, and she looked pleased.

I followed her outside and into the Jeep. It was too noisy to talk on our way to the stable, and when we pulled up, Candy Butler jumped out, pocketed her keys and mounted her waiting mare.

"I wanna get out there, see how bad it's hurt," she said to Pete. "Ride out with her to the hammock soon as you get her horse ready." She waved a hand at me, said "See you in a few," and galloped off to the north.

In a way, I was glad she'd gone ahead. That way, I didn't have to clamber awkwardly aboard with her watching.

Chapter 17

Pete was good with horses, and he was fast. In ten minutes, he'd cinched up the saddle, settled the reins across the pommel and offered me a hand.

I put my left Top-Sider in the stirrup and swung the right one over the horse's back. Well, more or less; it took two tries. When I was settled, Pete mounted a mahogany-colored mare and trotted us off in the direction Ms. Butler had taken.

I'd done very little riding over the last twenty years, and it took awhile to get the feel again, but my horse was good natured and trotted along as happily as if I didn't exist. Ms. Butler's foreman did pretty much the same. Pete was either the strong silent type or he didn't find my company exhilarating. Silence was fine with me.

The sun ducked in and out of the clouds, and I could see

extensive fields through breaks in the trees, mostly grazing land studded with scrub palmettos and the occasional swampy swale. We appeared to be heading for a good-sized group of trees that was probably the hammock Ms. Butler referred to. It looked a long way for a foal to have strayed by itself.

We'd been riding about ten minutes when Pete's cell phone rang. He pulled up his horse, listened and turned to me.

"Candy needs a hypodermic. She says for you to come ahead to the hammock. She calls it a hammock, but it's really a pine cluster. Keep riding straight at it — five minutes maybe. You'll see her off to the south side with the colt. I'll get the medicine and be right behind you."

He wheeled around and began a slow gallop back toward the ranch buildings. Marlborough man in action. I had to admit, he looked good riding away.

The sun had begun to fade at some point. I looked at my watch, saw ten 'til four, and realized there were less than two hours before sunset. Maybe not even that, since storm clouds had massed off to the west while I wasn't paying attention. They were moving fast, clustered like a dirty grey, elongated animal, head thrust out, claws stretched to grab at you.

I picked up a little speed, but after several minutes I didn't see any trace of either Ms. Butler or a baby horse. The hammock, or whatever it was, had resolved itself into scrubby pine trees, banked with overgrown grass and bushes. Not the nice woods you meandered through up north, just a jungle of impassable vegetation, and God knew what kind of crawly things.

I was beginning to get uneasy. Maybe Pete had said north end, not south. I pulled the horse around and rode in the other direction, calling out Ms. Butler's name.

Nobody answered.

The storm, massive and swifter moving than I'd realized, was crowding out the sun. In the west, a jagged streak of light cut a vertical line through the black and purple sky. The clatter of thunder that immediately followed meant the lightening was close, if I remembered my fifth-grade science. Damn. Here I was, stuck in an open field with a storm coming, and no shelter. Anyone who lives in Florida knows what a stupid move that is.

There was a path that somebody had apparently cut into the trees, and not too long ago, since hunks of palmetto and grass littered the ground at its opening. As I debated, a blinding flash of white lit the entire sky. This time, thunder shook the ground, the horse and me. It sounded like a thousand steel pans tumbling down a staircase. I held the reins tightly and eyed the path. Going into the trees probably wasn't the smartest move, but it would be better than standing out in the storm like a freaking flag pole. I turned the horse toward the opening, ducking down to miss the overhanging branches.

"Ms. Butler? Are you in here?"

Something buzzed by my head as I leaned forward, peering into the undergrowth. Half a second later I heard the follow-up sound that identified the buzz as a gunshot.

My horse, not skittish at all before, abruptly bolted and tossed me headfirst into a scratchy patch of saw grass. It was a perfect B-movie pratfall, and it might have been funny if it hadn't hurt. I picked my way out of the stickers and tried to catch the horse, but my efforts were uninspired and short-lived since he'd already disappeared down the path.

I was now on foot, scratched, bleeding and miles from civilization. Oh, yeah, and threatened by a monster storm. Before I could start whining for real, another shot pinged into a nearby tree, and I charged down the makeshift path into the undergrowth.

There were bugs in the bushes, and the storm clouds had turned the hammock dark as night. When I heard another shot, I ran until there was no breath left in me, until the path was gone and the grass was higher than my knees. The hammock hadn't looked that big when I was riding toward it. Now it seemed endless.

The next flash of lightning illuminated the sky through the lacey treetops overhead. The trees didn't give as much protection as I'd expected, and rain came down like the gods were dumping it out of buckets. I turned around in circles, wiping rain from my eyes, looking for a way out. Unfortunately, I have no sense of direction. Just move! my own voice screamed in my head. *Take any damned direction at all!*

I was way past panic. The whole place was seriously spooky. Post-millennium Florida didn't exist here, just insects, swamp and lurking reptiles. Maybe even the ghosts of ancient Seminole warriors bent on revenge. Maybe even bears.

It seemed like hours before I rediscovered the path leading out of the hammock. I was moving along it as fast as possible, skirting tree roots and sticker bushes, when something hideous materialized between me and the way I wanted to go. In the near-darkness, a fat, bloated shape oozed up out of the ground and stretched to a long, narrow tube. It was a snake, a thick, black one, squishing up out of its hole — bulge and ooze, bulge and ooze — before it angled to the ground and slithered away.

A scream caught in my throat, and I backpedaled several feet before I tripped and went sprawling.

". . . need help?" It was a man's voice, and I caught only the last two words as I scrambled to my knees and peered through the weeds. Something was coming. The dark outline of a horse and rider, ominous and huge, appeared on the path in front of me. There was something wrong with the rider, something misshapen in the area around his waist. I stayed where I was, pretending he couldn't see me, waiting for another gunshot.

A flash of lightening lit the man's baseball cap, jeans and checkered shirt. It turned the black shadow at his waist into a baby calf draped across the neck of the horse as if it had thumbed a ride. Both calf and rider seemed to be smiling at me. There was something luminous about them, the kind of aura produced by a hologram. Was it some kind of trick photography — some kind of incredible practical joke engineered to scare people away?

The rider lifted a checkered sleeve and pointed off to the left.

"That way. You're all right now."

The words carried to me, low and calm, in spite of the storm. But before I had a chance to react, rain came thudding down, white rain that frothed as it fell and reduced visibility to zero. The next time lightening lit the hammock, the rider and his hitchhiking calf were gone.

I got to my feet and followed the direction he'd indicated, holding on to bushes as I went. The wind kept roaring, gusting to a crescendo, then dropping to almost nothing, the way it does when a tornado is about to wipe out a few blocks of your hometown. Eventually, I reached the edge of the hammock and the dark, empty pasture land beyond it.

The guy on horseback was only a few yards away, headed again in my direction.

I began to melt back into the trees, then thought, What the hell. He could have riddled me with bullets when I was on the ground, but he hadn't. I'd rather be dead than spend the night in a creepy thicket. Well, kind of.

As the horse got closer, I saw the rider wasn't holding a gun. Or wearing a ball cap or carrying a calf. In fact, it wasn't him at all; it was Ms. Butler's foreman, Pete. I stumbled out of the shelter of the trees.

"My horse threw me." I managed to get out. It was like my throat had frozen shut.

"Are you all right?"

I could barely hear him over the rain. I rasped back. "Scratched up and freezing to death."

He nudged his mount closer. "Come here."

"Did you find my horse?"

"No, but mine can carry us both a ways." He leaned down and took my arm. "Stand on my boot."

Stand on his boot? Well, why not? I was too cold and miserable to argue.

Pete stuck out a foot, I stepped on top of it, and he swung me up and around behind his saddle in an easy motion. Then he stripped off his waterproof jacket and told me to put it on. It wasn't cozy but it did stop me getting any wetter.

"There's a flask in the pocket. Have a shot of that," he ordered.

I got it out and swallowed enough to make me cough before screwing the lid back on.

He spoke over his shoulder to me. "You'll have to hold on to me until we get back."

The jacket was so bulky, I left it open and stretched my arms around his waist. He was nearly as wet as I was, but he was very, very warm. Like a mini-heater. I pressed into his back as tightly as I could and relaxed as the warmth of the whiskey coated my stomach. The rain was still coming down, but now it blew sideways in stinging gusts. I buried my face in the back of Pete's neck.

Somebody had shot at me, but who? And why? If it was Pete, there was something seriously wrong with his organizational ability, because he appeared to be saving me. *Maybe*, a voice in my head suggested, *he's going to lock you in one of the barns.*

Terrific. I blanked out the voice because I was determined to be saved. And that made me think of the apparition on horseback, the one who'd pointed the way out of the hammock. He'd looked young, like a kid, but there was something wrong with him. Not the bulge around his waist — that was the calf. Something about the eyes, something dark under the shadow of his cap.

Oh, shit. I clung tighter to Ms. Butler's ranch foreman and shuddered. The guy had been wearing a mask — a freaking Lone Ranger mask.

The slow ride from the hammock to the ranch probably took half an hour, but it seemed I'd been holding on to Pete forever. I stayed attached to him even as we reached the first of the ranch buildings.

"Where's Ms. Butler?" I said to the back of his ear.

"She was in the barn."

A couple of seconds later, a tall figure came out of one of the stables and walked toward us.

Pete reached around to help me down from the horse, then dismounted himself.

"Where the hell were you?" Candy Butler was wearing expensive, foul-weather gear, which looked nearly dry. "I've been back for an hour, doctored the foal and had a beer besides."

"Yeah?" My voice was flat. "Good for you. How'd you get the foal all the way back here?"

She stared at me. "How? Across the front of my saddle. Like always."

That jolted me. Just like the Lone Ranger's calf. "You take a rifle out there with you?"

"Certainly. There's always one on my saddle. Why?"

"Somebody shot at me while I was looking for you. Three times."

"Shot at you?" She glanced at the foreman, and if she'd said, "Wacko," and spun her finger in a circle around her ear, the meaning couldn't have been clearer. "You didn't hear a shot, did you, Pete?"

He shook his head slowly.

"Must have been thunder or a crack of lightening or something. Nobody in their right mind would be hunting out there in this storm. Anyway, the land's posted. Nobody allowed." She turned to the foreman. "Better get her inside and pour a drink in her. I'll find some dry clothes."

"No thanks," I took off Pete's jacket and handed it to him. "I have to get home. I have an . . . an appointment."

Ms. Butler threw back her head and laughed. "I thought you were going with me to that trailer."

"Not now."

"At least put on some dry clothes; you'll catch your death," she protested, but I was already heading for my car.

When I finally got there, I jabbed my shaking key in the ignition and started the engine.

Candy Butler had apparently followed me on foot. She walked up and pounded on my window.

I rolled it down two courtesy inches and peered at her as rain blew in on my face.

"I hope this doesn't mean you're quitting on me," she snapped. "You need to toughen up . . . and you can stitch that one on a pillow. There's a lot more to do. That . . . onion picker you found probably isn't Bobby at all —"

I rolled up the window, effectively cutting her off, put the car in reverse and backed the entire length of her approach road at a solid thirty miles an hour. Fortunately, the gates were open, because I wasn't in any mood to stop. When I hit the highway, I whipped the car in a reverse circle, locked all my car doors and flew home, heater turned so high it steamed the windshield.

Chapter 18

The rain had finished by the time I pulled up in front of the house, but it was pitch dark outside. My watch had quit working, and I couldn't even guess the time. It felt like midnight.

My hands had stopped shaking on the drive home. Pete's whiskey and the car heater had probably saved me from going into shock. The closer I got to Seminole Beach, the more unreal the experience at the Butler Ranch seemed. My brain bounced the word improbable around in the warm, darkened car long after the adrenalin rush wore off: improbable, improbable, im-prob-a-ble. After that, it was just a short hop to unbelievable and from there to impossible. The last two miles I wasn't afraid anymore, just tired enough to drop.

When I walked in the back door, Bear and Kenji were eating dinner at the worktable in the kitchen. At midnight? I glanced at the microwave clock and saw it was only twenty past eight.

"What happened to you?" Amy turned from the stove and eyed my muddy, crumpled hair, jeans and jacket.

"A horse threw me. I'm going up to shower."

"Here, take this with you." She handed me her glass of wine. "Dinner's Bahamian chicken boil. Lots of garlic. You look like you need it."

The shower was hot and stung my face and hands. I began to feel the bruises I'd picked up rolling around in Candy Butler's pine cluster. I sprayed Bactine around indiscriminately, donned a pair of sweat pants, a hooded shirt and thick socks and went back downstairs. There was a time when I'd have crawled in bed with a heating pad and pulled a blanket over my head. But to-night, I wanted soup and more wine and the company of people who didn't want to shoot me.

The Bahamian chicken boil had garlic all right, also white chicken, potatoes, onions, broth and lime juice. I started feeling better by the third spoonful.

Nobody said anything about my scratched-up face, and Bear held off on questions until I'd nearly finished eating.

"So, did Ms. Butler identify the picture as her son?" he said, finally, patience exhausted.

I put down the spoon. "She wasn't sure. She was going to the trailer to see him but went to check out a missing foal first. I rode along — more or less."

I told them the rest of the story, but left out the snake and the fact that I was so terrified I stuck like a leach to Candy But-ler's foreman for half an hour.

"So," Bear said slowly. "Ms. Butler had a rifle. You think she shot at you?"

"She could have, but why?"

Kenji poured more wine in my glass. "Maybe foreman does the shooting?" he offered.

"Then why come looking for me and bring me back?"

"Maybe it was just a warning," Bear said, frowning. "I mean, was somebody actually trying to hit you?"

"Geez, Bear, I don't know. I was too busy crawling out of sticker bushes to delve into the shooter's motivation. Did the shots sound close? Yeah, two of them did."

"The reason I asked was, with a rifle, you have to be accurate within a mile to actually hit something. With a twenty-two, it's a lot closer. A shotgun's good for maybe eighty yards, but you'd know because it scatters. You see anybody around at all?"

"Not until the masked man with the calf turned up."

"That's really the part I don't understand." Bear got up and began pacing the kitchen floor. "Who'd be riding around Candy Butler's back forty in the middle of a thunderstorm?"

"In a Lone Ranger mask," I reminded him.

"Right. You didn't recognize the guy at all?"

I shook my head. "But he had young, really smooth cheeks and he looked — I don't know . . . really happy? Serene. Something like that."

"Probably just a whack job," Amy said. "They all end up in Florida."

Bear stopped pacing. "You positive it wasn't the foreman? He was right there when you came out of the trees."

"It wasn't him."

Kenji made a clearing sound in his throat. "You are sure it was a man?"

For some reason, a little frisson went up my back. "I thought so."

"Maybe it was a woman dressed like a guy," Amy suggested.

"We have smoother faces. Especially in the dark —"

"Okay, here's the deal," Bear interrupted. "Tomorrow we go out to Lost River and report this to the sheriff. You haven't called them, right?"

"No, I just wanted to get the hell out of there. But Ms. Butler obviously didn't believe me. They probably wouldn't either."

"Doesn't matter," Bear said. "We'll report it on principle."

On principle? I stared at him, wondering what he was up to, then shrugged, suddenly too tired to care. I looked around the table. "Where's everybody else?"

"Lee Lee took Jesse out for vegetarian pizza, and Maggie's apparently sleeping. Amy took her some soup, but the door's locked, and she's not answering again." Bear's mouth thinned in disapproval. "We'll take her with us tomorrow. Get her out of the house."

When I went up to bed a few minutes later, I intended to sleep until noon the following day. Unfortunately, I'd planned without Detective Christensen, who came banging on the door at eight a.m. with intentions of his own.

Christensen's dark hair was messy, he hadn't shaved and he was wearing an "I have no sense of humor and this is not a friendly call" face. It didn't take long to discover the reason: Just after midnight, somebody had stumbled across a man's body on the outskirts of Lost River. The man had literally been shot off his bicycle, and after several hours, he was identified as Carlos Moscala. His live-in girlfriend gave deputies the description of a pushy couple who came to her trailer asking questions two days earlier.

The detective looked me over, from the top of my head to my sock feet.

"She was a good describer. I recognized you immediately,

except she didn't mention all the scratches." When I didn't respond, he said, "You knew we were looking for them, and you said you didn't know who they were. You want to tell me who you took with you to interfere in my investigation?"

I swallowed a yawn and nodded. "If you wait a second, I'll go get him."

Christensen wouldn't wait. He insisted on accompanying me to the third floor to wake up Bear, who wasn't thrilled to see the law but was at least wearing jockey shorts when he opened the door. He pulled on a pair of jeans and followed us down to the kitchen.

While Detective Christensen sucked down several cups of Amy's Italian roast, Bear explained how he'd discovered the whereabouts of Red, Porky Joe and Carlos Moscala, and we related our conversation with them at the trailer. Neither of us mentioned my idea that Porky Joe and Bobby McCleod might be the same person. The detective was clearly in no mood for speculation from the likes of us.

Bear did say that somebody had shot at me the night before at the Butler Ranch — probably with a rifle — but Christensen only looked skeptical and asked if I'd reported it. Then he demanded to know what I'd been doing out there anyway. I gave him the short version — riding around Candy Butler's ranch while she looked for a foal — and he looked even more dubious.

About that time, Lee Lee came wandering downstairs in search of coffee. Christensen recognized her, of course, and when he realized she'd been staying in the house since Stubb's murder, he got annoyed all over again.

"I told you before, Mrs. Shaw, everybody in front of that church is a suspect in Flanders' death. It doesn't matter whether you were all in sight of each other during the critical times. Somebody could have been hired to kill the guy." He turned to Bear. "And I still don't understand why you were so interested in three field-workers. Why track them down, let alone take them a bottle of whiskey . . ."

"I was the one who took Bear along," I interrupted. "He felt sorry for the guy — for Joe. The guy was a shaky mess." I hesitated as he continued to stare at me. Telling him the truth, that Ms. Butler wanted me to investigate Stubb's death, sounded ridiculous, even to me.

"Candy Butler asked me to try to find her son," I said, finally, staying within the letter of the truth, "and there was a chance those guys knew something."

His eyes narrowed a little. "Is that something you do, Mrs. Shaw? Find people?"

"Not really. Ms. Butler and I have a mutual friend, and he suggested she call me."

Christensen didn't look like he believed that either, but when I told him the friend was Tom Roddler, our probable next state representative, he turned thoughtful, made a few notes and motioned Lee Lee, who'd been leaning against the sink, to a seat at the table.

"You two want to be careful if you head out to Lost River again," he warned, waving Bear and me out of the room. "Somebody out there's running around with a gun."

Lee Lee's interview was probably the shortest on record because the detective was back in his car in less than fifteen minutes. Bear and I stood on the front porch, watching as he pulled away from the curb.

"She probably sang all her answers, and he couldn't take it," Bear said with a wry grin. Then, "Why didn't he tell us to cease and desist immediately? We were talking to Carlos two days before he got offed."

"Because he wants to keep an eye on us?"

Bear doesn't know it, but his eyes get bluer when he's honestly worried. "If he's really thinking hired killer, he'll be all over our bank records. Never mind interrogating friends to see if we ever mentioned wanting Stubb dead. We're going to have to settle down and figure out who really did this. C'mon, I've got an idea for a relationship grid, and Maggie dug out a boatload of good shit about Father Mike yesterday. Let's get on it."

Instead of trailing him dutifully upstairs, I walked down to the river, sat on the seawall and tried to decide what to do, if anything. It was cold for Florida, maybe sixty-five degrees, and good thinking weather. God knows we don't get enough of that.

Bear has never solved anything, in spite of his exhausting zeal. He gathers information efficiently enough, but we disagree totally on how to interpret it. His writer's mind jumps to far-out scenarios. For me it's just a question of listening, waiting for one piece of data to click with another, and watching for the actual truth instead of what passes for it. And that's not being psychic, it's just how the subconscious mind works. Unfortunately, I seemed to be short on data at that moment — and even shorter on enthusiasm.

My cell rang. It was Tom Roddler's number, and I hesitated about two seconds before picking it up.

"What?"

"I wondered if you were ever going to talk to me again. Want to meet for a drink or dinner — or anything else?"

"No."

"What's going on, Keegan?" His voice was so warm and concerned, I'd have called it loving if it belonged to anybody else.

"Well, let's see, the police just left. That was fun. Otherwise, nothing good since you gave your friend, Candy Butler, my name. Why would you do something like that?"

I could almost hear him thinking. "She seemed to need some help? It *is* the kind of thing you do."

"It is not. I'm a photographer, not a freaking reporter, and I don't like messing in other people's business, even for money. And particularly not in hers. She's too dark, she gives me the creeps."

More silence. Then, "What did the police want?"

"Don't you read the papers? Two guys in Lost River got murdered. I happened to be in front of St. Jude's when they found the first guy, and I'd spent some time with the field-worker somebody shot last night. They've questioned practically everybody in the house, and even Bear's worried. Not that he should be. They can look through our bank accounts 'til their badges fall off without finding personal checks to hit men."

"Sounds like I've landed you in it without meaning to."

"Sounds like." I brushed a hand across my forehead. The truth was, I was more concerned about Maggie than anybody else. If Christenson found out she was in town — actually at the church the night Stubb died — and had opened a window without setting off the alarm . . .

"It's such a mess, I can't even think what to do."

"I'm sorry, Keegan, really. Stay calm, you'll figure it out. Somebody knows something, left something out or held it back for whatever reason. They always do. In the meantime, I'll see what sort of interference I can run on my end."

After we disconnected, with no more talk of meeting for a drink, I sat and continued looking at the river. Talking to Tom had actually been comforting, but I didn't let it go to my head —

I mean heart. Reid would be here soon. He was much better for me than a guy who let selfish interests interfere with our fragile emotional connection.

That was such a mouthful, and so pretentious, I couldn't help grinning. I stood up and told myself to quit wallowing in self-indulgent crap. Time to go see what Bear was up to in his incident room.

Chapter 19

Bear was busy being annoyed. He gets like that when you don't follow his orders immediately and without question. A second piece of shelf paper had been taped to the wall under the first, and thick black circles, with lines jutting out to smaller circles, filled most of it. He was totally engrossed in putting names in each of the circles. Apparently, this was the relationship grid he'd been talking about, but it looked like a collection of aberrant sunflowers.

It was a good ten minutes before he acknowledged my presence and then only because he was dying to explain his brilliant idea. His blue eyes narrowed as he expounded on who knew who, how they knew them and how they were all related to Stubb's death.

When I listened dutifully and refrained from negative remarks of any kind, Bear got even more expansive.

"You'll never guess what Father Mike Durkin did in Boston to get himself exiled to Florida," he said, slapping a printout into my hand.

"Little boys, little girls or just consenting adults?" I said, obscurely disappointed in Father Mike.

"Worse."

"What could be worse?"

Bear shrugged. "Murder? Father Mike has cousins in Northern Ireland. In the nineteen eighties, he helped them raise money to buy guns for the Irish Republican Army. He was also present when a car filled with automatic weapons arrived in the church parking lot during a prominent Boston wedding."

"Whoa." I studied the printout. "A trunk-load of nine-millimeter pistols, M-sixteen rifles and a hundred thousand rounds of ammunition? All stolen from U.S. Marine bases?"

Bear nodded. "But something went wrong at the church. A known IRA member was shot dead, and the money and guns disappeared. The police arrested everybody in the vicinity, including the mother of the bride. Father Mike got bailed out of jail next day and disappeared. Four months later, he was transferred to the Palm Beach Diocese and then to Lost River, Florida."

"He was smuggling guns, and the church didn't boot him?"

"C'mon, Keegan, they reassigned pedophiles for years. What do they care about one lousy gun runner?" Bear rubbed his chin, which needed shaving. "But he would make a great character, a fallen priest, overwhelmed by guilt, a little elicit sex thrown in . . . struggling to integrate inexplicable evil with necessary evil . . ."

Blessedly, my cell phone rang. It was Candy Butler.

"I want to apologize for last night," she said. "I've been tired and bent out of shape for a couple of days, and I was too hard on you. I'm thinking we ought to just let this whole thing go. I found the house you were talking about, but that Joe guy doesn't live there anymore. Then some sheriff's deputy traced him to Palm Beach, where he got picked up on a DUI. They asked me to come down and identify him, and I went, but it wasn't Bobby. Looked a little like him, but . . . Listen, this whole thing's got out of hand. The cops are pissed off, and I'm sorry I was short with you last night . . ."

When she finally stopped for a breath, I said, "So, you don't want me to look around anymore? You're not worried Christensen will try to pin Stubb's murder on you?"

"Well, not so much now, I guess. Living with suspicion isn't that hard once you get used to it, and I've had practice. They'll either find out who did it or they won't, and I guess I can live with that too. I'm putting a check in the mail to you —"

"Don't do that," I interrupted. "I didn't do anything to earn it."

"Already done. See ya." She hung up.

I put down the phone, all kinds of alarms going off in my head. I didn't think it was like Candy Butler to quit or apologize, and she was doing both. The fact that I didn't want to have anything to do with her got shouldered aside by the need to know what she was up to.

Bear was regarding me with genuine amusement. "Dumped you, huh?"

"Like a heavy rock in shallow water." I started out the door.

"Where are you going?"

"Not sure." I half turned. "Did you check Maggie's phone to see if the sheriff's department's tried to get in touch with her? They must have Stubb's cell; they should have traced her number by now."

When Bear went to check on Maggie's old messages, I slipped out of the house.

Chapter 20

I'm not sure what took me back to Gail Meyerson's. My intention was to look up Candy Butler, but somewhere on the way out, Mrs. Meyerson's face popped into my mind, along with Tom's remark about people holding back information, and the BMW kind of went in that direction all by itself.

Mrs. Meyerson met me at the door of her trailer wearing a green velour sweat suit and white running shoes and, as before, we sat on her glassed-in porch. But this time she was not as welcoming, and there were no cookies.

"I probably shouldn't be talking to you at all," she said, crossing her arms across her chest. Her face looked even more wrinkled than I remembered. "I don't want Ms. Butler saying I've been gossiping behind her back. She's not somebody you want on your bad side."

"I understand," I assured her, "but she's the one who put me on to you to begin with. Anything I can find out about Bobby might help locate him." I eyed her rigid chin and manipulated the truth some more. "She'll be grateful to anybody who helps her find the only family she has left."

After a long thirty seconds, she uncrossed her arms and leaned back against the bentwood couch. "Well, all right, then, if it's her idea."

I took out a notebook, saw the uncomfortable look on her face and returned it to my shoulder bag. It wasn't like I needed it. I had no idea what to ask, and silence stretched out between us as I waited for inspiration. It had reached a seriously awkward level when the name Gil Butler popped into my head.

"Ms. Butler was telling me about her husband's accidental shooting a couple of days ago," I said. "She mentioned pulling her sons out of school and sending them to relatives. Do you remember that happening?"

"Oh, yes." Gail Meyerson continued to look uneasy. "They went to Illinois or maybe Indiana — one of the 'I' states. But just for a few months. They were back to start school in the fall."

"Ms. Butler said the boys were very upset, devastated, really."

"Well, Bobby was, but I think I told you before, he was the sensitive one. Scott just rolled with the punches. Bobby had a tendency toward depression, I always thought."

"They must have been very attached to their stepfather."

"Oh, I wouldn't say attached. In fact, I'd say they disliked him."

At my look of surprise, she shrugged. "He wasn't an easy man to like, and probably an impossible one to love. He drank, you know. Candy moved in with him when the boys were six or seven, but they didn't get married until later on. The word was that she saw him and his ranch as a way to support the twins.

Gil Butler's first wife died of a heart attack — some said from overwork — a couple of years before he met Candy. He didn't have any children of his own, and I expect that was by preference."

"Still, he took Candy's on?"

Mrs. Meyerson leaned forward, her reluctance to dish dirt forgotten. "Yes, but she was quite a looker back then, very feminine. Not the complete ranch woman she is now. And, of course, she was a tragic figure, given her past."

"How do you mean?"

"Why her first husband, Keith McCleod, the interior decorator."

"An interior decorator? In Lost River?" I tried not to sound incredulous.

"Well, he worked in Palm Beach, but he and Candy moved up here when the boys were babies. He commuted."

"What happened to him?

She held up a palm. "He . . . well, he just disappeared. Everybody knew about it. It was a big scandal at the time, but Candy's had her share of those. She was probably thirty-one, and he was a couple of years older. One day he didn't come home, and they found his car out at the locks. His clothes were all folded in a neat pile on the ground, and everybody assumed he jumped in the canal and drowned."

"Did they find the body?"

"No, and that caused talk too. Because a year or so later, some local car dealer was on vacation in Mexico and swore he saw Keith on a beach in Acapulco with some young stud type. I don't think anybody believed him. You know men, bigger gossips than women any day."

"Her marriages didn't last long, did they?" I said thoughtfully. "I mean, six or seven years to the designer, another six or seven to the rancher."

"No." A slight smile touched Gail Meyerson's mouth. "But her foreman's been around for years."

I looked at her expectantly. "And?"

"Why, nothing. Nothing in particular." Her eyes shifted away from me, and the words came out in a tangle. "I mean, she knew him back when her first husband disappeared. At nineteen. I mean he was nineteen. The foreman. He's like family, I guess. I think he even flies her plane."

And that was it; just like that, I'd lost her. She either knew some choice item about Pete Beck and Candy Butler, or thought she did. Either way, she wasn't telling me. After a few more awkward questions, I gave up, thanked her and drove slowly back through town.

I couldn't wait to get home and tell Bear about Ms. Butler's first husband, the decorator. He'd missed that completely in his undercover intelligence gathering. Unfortunately, a lot of people had decided to visit Lost River today, and I got held up in front of St. Jude's. Traffic came to a complete stop as dozens of cars attempted to find places to park.

I'd been sitting there for probably five minutes, drumming my fingers on the steering wheel, when I saw Elena, Stubb Flanders' favorite cleaning girl, duck out the side door of the church and disappear around back. I made an instant decision, angled across opposing traffic to a side street and parked the BMW in a patch of soft sand that everybody else had avoided for fear of getting stuck. Then I slammed the car door and darted behind St. Jude's.

Elena was having a cigarette break in practically the same spot where Stubb had been sitting the night he staked out the dirt room. She dropped the butt on the ground when I rounded the corner, then realized who I was and looked disgusted.

"What you want now?" Her dark eyes were not friendly.

This time I didn't make a mistake. I unzipped my shoulder bag, dug out twenty dollars and handed it over. "I want to know about the day Stubb made you clean the hallway and the back window."

"I said about that." She scowled at me, but she snatched at the bill. "He says everything is dirty, that even the alarm is greasy. I tell him we don' touch it since I spray the telephones and the whole system is — *se arvino!* — you know, wrecked. He says clean everything anyway."

"Okay. Were there stains on the walls or back of the side door? Anything unusual you noticed?"

Her head was shaking back and forth as she searched out another cigarette.

I pointed at the small window in the back wall of the church. "What about that? Any marks on the glass or on the wood around it?"

"Fingerprints. But they were his."

"His? Mr. Flanders'?"

"Yesss." She rolled her eyes and took an orange Bic lighter out of her pocket. "I said so. He was touching it, inside and out. He said to clean it. Then he said to clean it again."

"Really." I thought that over. "What about the burglar alarm? The key pad? Does it look exactly the same as it did before?"

"No." Her voice got huffy and one hand tightened into a fist. "Now it is clean."

I considered taking back my twenty bucks but decided I'd rather keep my teeth. Elena was one of those people you really, really don't want to piss off.

Chapter 21

I never got a chance to gloat over my news about Candy Butler's first husband, and it was awhile before I even got to pass it on. That's because 32 East River Road was in minor uproar mode when I walked in.

Kenji rarely disagrees with anyone, but he had pulled his wiry black hair into a pony tail with one hand and was waving the other as he paced the kitchen floor. He's learned to hold his own in an argument with Bear, but his English, always iffy when he's upset, often omits critical bits.

"You do not listen!" he was almost shouting, "Not shot, hit on head. Many times. That is hate, not money. You ignore priest who has most motive and those two from . . . Cedar Key. No one of name Eddie or Cara . . . Ortega lives in that town. Not on property or telephone records. Also did not stay at

Mikasuki Inn that . . . night, as they said to Lee Lee."

Bear, who gets cranky when he has to do menial labor, stopped applying putty — badly — to Amy's broken window and snapped, "How do you know that?

"Talked to the Inn. Someone . . ."

Lee Lee, sitting at the kitchen table with a cup of green tea, began to sing the lyrics to "Someone to Watch Over me."

Kenji flashed her an expressionless look. "The . . . Ortegas disappear following police interview."

"They were probably named to other people and didn't want to get involved." Bear's shrug was dismissive. "Lot of people in Florida lie about where they came from. Never mind where they're going. Anyway, anybody, including the Ortegas, could have hired somebody to knock off Stubb. Though, why you'd sit out front and wait for it to happen, beats me. The point I was trying to make is, we have to look for somebody who could afford to pay blackmail. A priest can't have much money. Ms. Butler probably does. I'm just saying."

"You don't know blackmail is there," Kenji protested, his English going further to pot, "only say because dead onion picker."

"A priest wouldn't do those things." Lee Lee interrupted with assurance, "particularly not Father Mike. I've talked to him lots of times; he's a lovely man."

Bear gave the window pane a thump. "Your *lovely man* once sold guns to the IRA and was involved in a fatal shooting in the nineteen eighties. Stubb Flanders knew and was prepared to spill it."

"Nobody cares about that old stuff anymore," she protested.

"Really? Then why did Father Mike bury himself alive in a place like Lost River?"

Lee Lee looked bored. "I think Kenji has the right idea. It's too weird that the Cedar Key couple showed up the same night Stubb decided to stake out the church. Maybe they were hanging around town waiting for him to show up."

"You saw them waiting around the town?" Kenji pounced on her. "You were there two nights also — at Mikasuki Inn. Yes? Before we met you . . . at the church."

"What?" I turned a sharp eye on Lee Lee. "You told me you'd just come in on the Miami bus."

"Busted." She gave me an apologetic grin. Her hair was fastened on top of her head and splayed out like a pale yellow flower with dark roots. "I did stay there. It cost every cent I had for those two nights, so when you offered me a room, it was a godsend. I didn't want you to think I was taking advantage, you know? I just wanted to hang out a little longer with all that healing energy."

"But you were so excited about the dirt," I reminded her, "You didn't say anything about seeing it before."

"Sorry." She smiled another apology. "I think I explain things really well, but other people don't seem to get it. I guess I'm a little hard to read sometimes."

"No kidding. Well, while I'm being confused, maybe you can clear this up. I meant to ask you before, but I got distracted. You went to high school in Seminole Beach, right? So you must have known Bobby and Scott McCleod."

Her eyes brightened. "Sure, I knew them. Why?"

"But you didn't notice Bobby sitting in the church yard the night Stubb Flanders was killed? At the picnic table when you went around back to see Stubb?"

"Of course not." She looked shocked. "Bobby and his brother were nice kids . . . those guys were bums. You sure it was him? I mean, if you and his mom were out beating the bushes for him, and he was there, underfoot, all the time —"

"How did you know I was looking for him?"

"I heard you guys talking about it. I mean, I wasn't listening or anything, but you can hear practically everything everybody says in this house." She sat up straighter in the chair. "Take me out to see the guy, and I'll tell you in two seconds if it's Bobby."

My bullshit detector was tuned to high alert but everything out of Lee Lee's mouth had the ring of her own slightly spaced-out truth.

"He seems to be missing," I said after a moment. "Nobody's seen him since Bear and I talked to him at the trailer. It's possible he's in West Palm Beach in jail, but —"

"Might be the best place for him." Lee Lee's vagueness disappeared, and her eyes expressed nothing but concern. "If one of those three guys saw the murderer, they probably all did. I hope somebody doesn't shoot the rest of them."

So did I. I turned to Bear, who had stopped trying to fix the window. "By the way, Bobby's not the first McCleod to disappear unexpectedly. His birth father did the same thing when Bobby was very young, only with a little more of a . . . splash."

Lee Lee started humming a few lines from "Splish, Splash," but I tuned her out and repeated Gail Meyerson's story about the pile of clothes by the canal. I had just reached to the part about Mexico when my cell phone rang.

It was Pete Beck. I recognized his voice the minute he said, "I've been thinking about you."

I left the kitchen and walked down the hall to the front porch. There was no reason for Pete to call unless Ms. Butler had sicced him on me for purposes of her own. Maybe he just had fond memories of the half hour I'd stuck to his back in a wet shirt and was taking a shot.

I could have saved myself the trouble of finding a private place to talk because our conversation lasted less than a minute. He asked if I'd meet him for a drink at a bar halfway between Lost River and Seminole Beach at nine thirty that night, and when I decided I wanted to know what he wanted enough to venture out that late, he rang off. Not bad work for a guy with limited conversational skills.

The bar Pete suggested was called The Booby Trap. I'd been there once before on a Wednesday Ladies' Night, but the evening had ended in a near riot. That's what you get when you mix a male stripper — who forgets to take off his boots before his pants — with a pet python named Buddy, a roomful of intoxicated women and a fog machine.

Pete was sitting at the bar alone, but the bartender was close enough to lick his face. She had a long, thick, black braid draped over one bare shoulder and her boobs pushed against a red stretch bandeau at least one size too small.

"So, whadd'ya think?" Her dark eyes were half-closed. "My ex says he'll straighten out and buy me a condo on the beach if I take him back. You think I should give him another chance?"

I didn't get to hear the answer because he turned just then and saw me.

The bartender, whose name tag said Mindy, looked put out.

Pete had good bar manners. He stood up, adjusted my stool a little closer to his and asked what I'd like to drink.

I started to say white wine, but changed to beer when I saw the huge chalkboard sign hanging behind the bar: Lorena Bobbit Contest Saturday. Free entry. Prizes!

Mindy stopped flapping her eyelashes at Pete and drew my Coors as if it caused her physical pain.

"What's the Lorena Bobbitt contest?" I said to her.

She shrugged and slapped the mug in front of me. "We line up hotdogs on the edge of a card table out back. When it's your turn, you run to the table, hands behind your back, grab a dog with your teeth, high-tail it across the yard and fling it in the bushes. One who throws it the farthest wins."

"Really. You get a lot of people willing to do that?"

"Hell, yes. They come up from Lauderdale for this one."

Pete picked up his bottle of Corona and saluted me: "To riding at night." His hair was ruffled and he needed a shave, but his smile was damned near irresistible.

I took a sip and looked straight into his dark, amused eyes. For a second, I was back on the horse, arms wrapped around his waist, face pressed into his shoulder. Heat crept through my body, and I was pretty sure it wasn't the beer.

"I haven't thanked you for saving me," I murmured. "It was creepy as hell out there. And a long walk back to Ms. Butler's house."

"My pleasure."

I took another sip of my beer. "So, uh, what's going on?"

Mindy was rinsing out glasses but still within hearing distance.

Pete opened his mouth, then stopped and shifted his gaze to her. After a few seconds, she looked up, dried her hands on a towel and fluffed off down the bar.

Impressive. I'd have to get him to teach me how to do that.

He looked down into his beer. "I wanted to tell you — don't come out to Lost River anymore."

I gaped at him. "Excuse me? Are you warning me off?"

"No, it's just better right now. Lot going on out there.

You've been asking a lot of questions. Smarter to stay away 'til everything dies down. No point asking for trouble."

He was still studying the contents of his glass, but I kept my eyes on what I could see of his face.

"That's a lot of reasons. What is it you know that I don't?"

He shook his head. "Just don't want to see anything happen to you."

"You did hear shots out by the hammock, didn't you? During the storm?"

"No." His head went slowly back and forth. "But some guy got it this morning at the edge of town. Gotta be careful."

I nodded. "I heard about that. A guy named Carlos Moscala. Did you know him?"

He shook his head.

We had another drink each, and I asked more questions, but Pete's responses were mostly limited to "No," "Nope" and "Uh-uh."

There's not much you can do with conversation like that. Eventually, I slung my purse strap over one shoulder and turned to face him. "Thanks for the drinks."

He nodded and handed me a folded bar napkin.

"What's this?"

"My cell number." He reached out a hand and pushed a strand of blonde hair behind my ear. "You call me, you need anything. Okay? Anything at all."

Again, I felt warmth invade my body. Who needs conversation when you can communicate with heat? Maybe it was working with those animals all day long. I stood up, looked into his eyes for a couple of long seconds and tore myself away.

As I went, I heard Mindy say to him, "You got a thing for

blondes, huh? At least this one doesn't have roots out to her eyebrows."

I was halfway to the front door when I saw the bartender from the Whole Hog, the one who supposedly had a fling with Pete before Ms. Butler told her to get lost. She was sitting alone at a table for two and skewered me with furious eyes as I passed.

I turned for a last look at Pete Beck. The Butler foreman was a busy guy. Imagine having enough energy to juggle a more than willing bartender, a blonde — with roots — and box cutter girl, all at the same time. Not to mention Candy Butler, who was no light weight at all.

Just as well I was heading home.

Chapter 22

Once Bear gets an idea in his head, it can only be removed by surgery or back hoe. He was convinced that Carlos Moscala had been shot for blackmailing somebody, although he wasn't sure who. He was also convinced that Stubb had been dispatched by the same gun. But his wildest supposition was that the gun that had done all the dispatching was hidden somewhere on Candy Butler's ranch. When I came downstairs for coffee around nine o'clock the next morning, he had abandoned relationship grids and become an expert on local ranch land.

Kenji, who disagreed with all of Bear's conclusions, nevertheless remained loyal. He had downloaded a mountain of data from the county tax assessor's website, and the two of them had used an entire roll of clear tape to piece it together. The result was an unwieldy, hexagonal guide to Ms. Butler's 240-acre ranch and the three properties that adjoined it. Taped to the edges of this masterpiece were aerial views of grazing land bordered by thickets of oak, pictures of horses and cattle, and photos of buildings and fences in various states of repair.

Bear thought it was brilliant.

To me, it looked like the work of a third grader on speed.

Ordinarily, Maggie would have functioned as cutting and taping expert, but she was in her room with the door locked again. When I asked why, Bear growled something that might have been "relapse," said he was handling it and to leave her alone.

"So, here's the deal." He finished highlighting drainage ditches on the Butler property. "Candy Butler's place is small because she started out raising draft horses, which takes less land than other kinds of ranching. Three properties border hers: two much bigger ranches and a riding stable. The stable," he paused to see if everyone grasped the concept, "rents out horses. So around noon, we drive out there, rent horses, ride the Butler property line and accidently stray over it. If we fan out and search all the likely spots, there's a good chance we'll find the weapon."

"When you say 'we'," Amy said, from in front of the sink. "Who, exactly, does that mean?"

Bear looked surprised "You, me, Kenji and Keegan."

"You've been breathing tape fumes. I don't ride horses. And Kenji's teaching a class today."

Kenji, whose idea of true American life involves reruns of *Dallas* and *Walker, Texas Ranger*, looked disappointed.

"Dark is better," he urged. "Ms. Butler . . . will call police if she sees everyone on her land."

"No, she won't. And the longer we wait, the more chance

somebody moves it." Bear frowned at him. "Okay, how about this. Keegan calls and reserves a couple of horses, and she and I go have a look. If we don't find anything, all four . . ." he glanced at Amy, "three of us go back tonight."

I refrained from saying it was stupid idea based on faulty reasoning and merely shook my head no. "I've already been thrown off a horse this week."

"I figure you owe me," Bear said without looking up.

Oh, yeah? I opened my mouth to say I was already paying him for Maggie, then remembered a number of things he'd done for me over the last few years. After a couple of seconds I sighed and reached for my cell phone. "What's the stable number?"

SunRidge Stables consisted of two long, tin-roofed barns with twenty-four boarded horses per building. The stalls were roomy and floored with fresh pine bark. A fancy dark green tack locker flanked each stall door.

The owner, a thin, dark-haired woman in jodhpurs, met us as we got out of the car.

"Your horses are saddled and ready to go," she told Bear. "We've got eighty acres of trails and an obstacle course. You want a guide? Or just a map so you can go it alone?"

Bear turned on his Hemingway grin, along with considerable charm, assured her we were experienced riders and asked about a place to eat a picnic lunch. As we mounted up, she waved us toward a wide path through some nearby trees.

"You'll see a lot of oak hammocks and pine clusters out there. In the hammocks, the trees shade out the underbrush so you can ride through easily. Just watch the low branches. But stay away from the pine clusters, too much brush and saw grass.

You'll cut up the animals' legs in there."

"How can we search them if we can't ride into them?" I complained, but Bear was already out of earshot, headed for the soft sand path.

My mount was a solid, personable two year old named Bathalsur, with a long, sensitive face and such gentle presence, I forgot all about being thrown off. The weather was near-perfect: sunny with a lot of feel-good blue sky and the kind of clouds they call mare's tails. That seemed appropriate.

After a couple of miles, I trotted up closer to Bear. "You really have a picnic lunch in that backpack?"

"Nope." He admitted, over his shoulder. "Folding metal detector."

"Ah, that improves the odds of finding anything at all. How far to the edge of the Butler property?"

"Four, maybe five miles. We head straight west."

"You realize that the police already searched her place. Even took the clothes she was wearing at the church that night. What could be left that they didn't find?"

"The gun that killed Stubb Flanders."

"He was killed with his own camera tripod."

"You say that because there was blood on it, but the papers never said a tripod made the bloody mark on his forehead."

"They never said a gun did either. We'd have heard a shot. We were sitting right out front."

"Ever heard of a silencer?" When I didn't answer, he went on. "Anyway, I don't believe they searched the Butler ranch just to get the clothes she wore that night. Everything seems to be centered around her property. There has to be something hidden there that leads directly to the killer."

As I said, when Bear gets an idea . . .

"So," I said, with weighty sarcasm, "we gallop wildly onto the Butler property, search frantically for metal objects that might have killed Stubb Flanders — even though we don't know exactly what they are — then get the hell out before somebody sees us trespassing and shoots us? That's the plan?"

"Sounds better every time I hear it," he said with a laugh.

Bear's good mood lasted until we reached the Butler ranch and came face to face with an eight-foot, commercial chain-link fence with barbed wire on top, the kind you see in pictures of the Mexican border. It meandered for miles in both directions, and it was obvious to me that all 240 acres of the Candy's property was fenced in or off, depending on your point of view.

"Thing's too damned high to jump." Bear growled as we stared through the links of the fence.

I kept my thoughts to myself. The last time he'd mounted an expedition, we'd ended up in a motorboat on the river, dodging shotgun fire. Still, that trip had been a success. This time, short of employing wire cutters or dropping in by parachute, we were finished before we started.

We could see a hammock or a pine cluster, or whatever they called it, less than a mile away on the other side of the fence. It sat there, tantalizing and out of reach. I wondered if it was the one I got lost in and how many there were. Probably too many to search. Supposing there was anything to find.

Bear rode up and down the fence line for the next ten minutes, looking like Steve McQueen in a sulk. Finally, he flapped a come-along hand at me and trotted back the way we'd come. He was either thinking deep thoughts or totally bummed. Whichever, he refused to talk all the way back to the stable, let alone discuss theories.

I rode along, discussing them with myself. The police hadn't released the cause of Stubb Flanders' death, but I'd seen that bloody camera tripod, and Bear hadn't. I didn't buy the hired-killer theory either. I've never met any hired killers — that I knew about anyway — but I agreed with Kenji. Hitting somebody in the head over and over argues hate, not cold blooded execution. Stubb had pissed off a lot of people in Lost River, but nobody hated him enough to beat him to a pulp. Although Elena, the cleaning girl, might have whacked him for dissing her choice of spray cleaner. She had that kind of face.

Back at the stable, I refrained from using the phrase "wild goose chase."

We took off the saddles and brushed down our horses to get the dried sweat out of their coats. I made sure Bathalsur had oats and water, rubbed his face for awhile and cooed to him. The smell and atmosphere of the place was beyond soothing. Two stable cats, one named Jesse and the other James, strolled around, meowing to have their chins rubbed. A third cat, a young white male with blue eyes and a mutilated, pus-filled ear, was more leery of strangers.

"The other cats don't like him," the owner admitted. "He's just an overgrown kitten, not really wild. I think he was a house pet, and somebody dumped him out here one night. He keeps hanging around, but they won't let him eat. And they beat up on him — you see his ear."

I held out the back of my hand, and eventually, the white cat edged close enough to let me scratch the undamaged part of his head. His fur was thick and soft, and he was going to be beautiful when he got older. If he got older. After awhile he rolled over on his side and stretched out so I could scratch his belly. I gave him a final pat and stood up. I wasn't in the market for another homeless waif. I had a houseful.

By the time we left the stables, Bear had apparently shrugged off the disappointment of a failed mission and was surprisingly upbeat. I was pulling out of the driveway onto the bumpy dirt road when I noticed an unnatural movement under his flannel shirt and stood on the brakes.

"What's wrong?"

"Your shirt . . ." I stopped, just as a white furry head poked up out of his top open button.

"No!" I snapped, and put the car in reverse. "We are not taking that animal home."

"C'mon, Keegan. Poor bastard'll starve if he stays here. He doesn't even understand why the other cats hate him."

"He's full of fleas. You'll be covered in them too. And so will my car."

"That's why I've got him in my shirt. When we get back, I'll give him and me and the shirt a bath. I'll even buy him a damned flea collar."

"You gonna walk him every day too?"

He grinned at me. "C'mon, Keegan . . . *now* what's wrong?"

I had stopped backing and was staring out the passenger window of my car into a humongous clump of trees and grass and bushes on the far side of the road. It looked like somebody had chopped a couple of yards of path into it, then given it up as a bad job.

"That's a pine cluster," I said to Bear. "Look behind you."

"Yeah?" He stared at me like I was a lunatic. "So?"

A whole bunch of isolated facts, things I'd heard or observed but failed to process, shifted in my head and settled into a totally different pattern.

I met Bear's blue eyes. "So this trip wasn't a waste of time after all. Your idea of searching Ms. Butler's property was spot-on."

"Of course it was, but we can't find the weapon if we can't . . ."

"There is no weapon, Bear. Well not exactly. I . . . let me think about it for awhile, okay?"

The look on his face said he thought I was blowing smoke, but I didn't care. I shifted into low gear and roared off down the dirt road, forgetting all about the cat. By the time we turned onto the main highway, I had decided how to find out if I was on the right track.

Bear never got around to giving the white cat a bath because Amy met us at the kitchen door with an update on Maggie.

"She finally came out of her room, but she's not talking. Just went up to Number Seven and looks terrible. I'm afraid she's going to do something to herself."

Bear and I went straight upstairs.

Maggie was in a chair, hands in her lap, eyes fixed on a blank computer screen. Wherever her mind was, it wasn't in the house. Maybe not even in Seminole Beach. I don't think she noticed when we entered the room.

Bear went over and stood beside her for a few seconds, then reached into his shirt and pulled out the overgrown kitten.

"Somebody dumped him out at the stables," he said, as if we'd just been discussing it. "The other cats wouldn't let him eat, and when he tried, they clawed his ear into an abscess." He put the animal in her lap and scratched at his own chest. "He's also got fleas. You think you could give him some milk or something?"

The kitten, upset at being handed around on top of his other troubles, tried to kick loose, but Maggie's hands had already closed around him. She lifted him to her shoulder, put a hand under his scrabbling feet and stroked the back of his head, murmuring comforting sounds. After awhile he stopped struggling, pressed his nose into her neck and stayed there.

"Cat's don't drink milk; it's not good for them," she said in a soft voice. Then she made a funny noise, got to her feet and stumbled from the room.

"Maggie?" I followed her out to the landing where she'd stopped at the top of the stairs. "Are you okay?"

She raised a face blurry with tears. "I can't see. I'm afraid I'll fall on the steps and hurt him."

"Come on." I went downstairs first and she followed in slow motion, clutching the kitten to her chest with one hand and the other on my shoulder. It was a very long time until we reached her room, and by then, Bear had gone to the kitchen and returned with a bowl.

"Amy cut up two boiled eggs for him," he said, setting the bowl on the wood floor. "She says that'll hold him until we get some cat food."

The kitten shied away until Maggie got down on her knees and gently guided his nose to the bowl. It was literally snorting chopped egg when Bear and I left.

Chapter 23

That was the high point of the day. The rest ranked right up there on the Life Sucks meter. After Maggie gave the white cat a bath, Bear drove her to the vet to see what could be done about its damaged ear. Kenji was still at his class in underwater photography, Jesse was holed-up in the porch studio with both doors closed, apparently having a relapse of his own, and Amy went on a grocery run in search of Welsh sea salt and fiddlehead ferns.

I was the only one in the house, with nothing to do except think, which wasn't working out.

When Lee Lee asked if I wanted to run the beach, I said no, but I should have made the effort. Or driven downtown for coffee or cleaned bathrooms or reshingled the roof. Instead, I wandered around in a fog, trying to figure out the details of Stubb's death. I was pretty sure I knew *who*, but I still didn't know *how*, which meant who didn't count.

At one point, I went to up to Number Seven, re-read the notes Kenji had posted on the wall and even studied Bear's weird relationship chart. All I learned was that the one person connected to every other person involved — was me. By three o'clock that afternoon, I was back in the kitchen, sipping my fourth cup of French roast, still unenlightened. *How the hell had Stubb got in the church without setting off the alarm?*

When Lee Lee wandered in, I was at the kitchen window, contemplating Bear and Kenji's failed superglue experiment. Bear hadn't replaced the panes to Amy's satisfaction, and she refused to clean it until he did. Grubby fingerprints covered the glass and the old-fashioned sash.

"What are you doing?" Lee Lee's hair was loose on her shoulders today, and her sky-blue eyes were bright with interest.

"Not sure. I think I'm thinking."

She nodded with absolute understanding and filled a kettle with water. "I do that all the time. Want some herb tea?"

"No. Thanks. How come you're not in Lost River? Soaking up vibes?"

She turned on the burner. "I don't know, it's kind of eerie with the police all over the place."

"That reminds me, what did Detective Christensen want when he talked to you yesterday?"

"Not much, really. He wanted to know how long I'd been here and how long I was going to stay. And where I lived and if I was born in Florida. And had I ever met Stubb Flanders before, stuff like that. I told him I hadn't met him and that I lived in Miami."

"Were you born in Florida?" I said, curious.

"Huh-uh. My family had a farm up in Tennessee. We moved to Seminole Beach when I was in high school and then on to Miami. My dad was a builder. But then he died." Her mouth turned down at the corners. "I hate it when people die."

I was getting used to Lee Lee's delivery style and let that one pass.

"You ever think about going back to Tennessee?" I said, wondering how long she intended to stay with us.

"Sometimes. I miss my dogs and the horses, but farms eat up all your money. We still have a little land up in the mountains . . ." She shrugged the thought away and shifted her attention to the computer on the worktable. Her fingers reached out to the keyboard.

"Amy writes her cookbooks on this, huh?"

"Between bouts of cooking."

"She should really clean it — these old light-colored keys are awful if you use them all the time. God, you can almost scrape off the grime. Talk about filthy . . ."

A stricken look appeared on her face. "I mean . . . I didn't mean it like that. Amy's so careful, keeps everything so clean and . . . well, people forget about their computers, don't they?"

I almost laughed out loud. For somebody who reveled in a room full of dirt, she was remarkably sensitive to just plain dirty.

She turned away from the kitchen table and rubbed her palms on her jeans. "Have you figured out who killed Mr. Flanders yet? Jesse says you solved two or three murders, and you can do anything, if you decide you want to."

"Jesse said that?"

Her blonde head bobbed enthusiastically, but I didn't believe it. It didn't sound like Jesse, for one thing, and he'd lost a girlfriend because of me, for another.

"Maybe it was just a robbery or something," she chattered on. "I know it couldn't be Father Mike. I see him every time I go there, and he's a really nice guy. Priests get such a bad rap these days, I mean they don't all do that stuff."

Something shifted in the back of my mind, more a feeling than an idea, something too tenuous to catch hold of. I stood motionless in the middle of the kitchen. I almost had it, one tiny obscure bit of information, trying to break through the clog of disassociated ideas in my head.

"Oh, damn it, damn it, I forgot something upstairs. I'll be right back." Lee Lee bolted out of the room, just as her teakettle started making boiling noises.

I turned off the kettle as it began to shriek and went back to the kitchen window, passing Amy's computer. The keyboard was as grubby as Lee Lee said, but not as bad as Bear's smudged prints on the kitchen window. I stared at the smudged fingerprints.

The kitchen phone shrilled in the quiet room, three, four, five times. That finished any attempt at critical thinking. I let the machine pick up, but whoever it was hung up on the dial tone. Damn, I needed to get the hell out of here. Too much noise, too much disruption. I went up to the mezzanine for my Nikes and a jacket.

Outside, the sun had been covered by a bank of clouds, and the breeze was cool and damp. I remembered the cloud formations Bear and I had seen at the stables. Mare's tail clouds, sooner or later, meant rain.

I was probably a block down the street when I heard Lee Lee calling my name, but I kept going. Any discussion with Lee Lee could wait. I trotted west, out of the neighborhood, breathing in and out like a yoga teacher had once taught me: Inhale the positives in life, release unneeded thoughts to the universe.

I'd covered several blocks, releasing the hell out of everything, when the thought of Stubb Flanders' treatment of Maggie refused to be relinquished. Why had she put up with his bullshit all these years? How could she be so clueless?

A block later, my righteous indignation turned on me. Was my relationship record that much better than Maggie's? First and worst, a married man with a homicidal wife. Next an alcoholic husband who smashed himself to pieces driving drunk. After that, a divorced guy who still hankered after his ex, followed by a hot-looking politician who was too old for me, followed by an ex-rocker who was probably too young for me, and several thousand miles away, besides. It was so depressing, I started counting out loud. You can't think when you count out loud. Fortunately, nobody in Seminole Beach walks anywhere, so nobody noticed.

The sun was gone, and it was getting dark before I realized I had wandered to the far side of Seminole Beach's fanciest shopping strip. If I went back the way I'd come, I was a good two miles from the house, but if I walked down the alley behind the stores and cut through a couple of backyards and one weedy, empty lot, I could knock off half a mile. I cut around behind the stores.

Alley is a misnomer for the space behind the Coral Reef shopping plaza. The backs of the stores have fake windows painted on them with real window boxes filled with blooming bougainvillea. All of the doors are flush with the walls, and the only garbage cans are two huge Dumpsters at either end of the passage. Even these are tasteful, with little green-and-white signs that read: *Inedible*. Which is only right in a place where the patrons drive cars worth more than some houses.

On the opposite side of the alleyway, an eight-foot, cement wall separated the plaza from the upscale gated community directly behind it. Every ten feet or so, the wall had a deep niche with iron bars set in vertically. Expensive flowering bushes had been planted on the subdivision side to keep gawkers from peering through the niches at homeowners. However, each recess was the height of the wall, and a foot wide by a foot deep, so if your eyes were good and you weren't overweight, you could squeeze in and eyeball the houses of the upper-middle class. Like everything else, it all comes down to size.

I was about two thirds of the way through the alley when the elusive thought I'd been chasing in the kitchen popped into my head like a dozen light bulbs lighting up at once.

I came to a dead stop, examining it from all angles. Surely that wasn't the explanation; it was too easy. Still, it explained why Stubb had been so picky about where and what Elena cleaned. It also explained how he'd gotten into the church undetected and probably how the murderer had slipped out.

At that moment, headlights flashed on behind me, and an engine started up. When I swung around, a vehicle, maybe fifty yards away, was coming straight at me. Fast.

Three thoughts registered simultaneously in my mind. One, the alley was just a little over one car wide. Two, there was nothing to duck behind. Three, I was likely to be pâté, if the car didn't stop.

It didn't. At the last minute, my body moved itself, scuttling sideways and leaping at the nearest barred niche. I pressed into the foot-deep recess, face flat against the bars.

The next second there was a roar, and a lot of heavy metal *whooshed* past my backside, accompanied by ear-splitting rap music. Something jerked the back of my jacket so hard, I was nearly pulled out of my bolt-hole.

I half fell, half jumped from the niche, staring stupidly after the taillights, until I saw the vehicle backing up, erratically, at great speed. This time, when I dived back in, I barely made it. A loud crunch accompanied the screech of brakes as a fender hit the wall, inches from my body. I pushed harder against the bars, and as Hemingway put it, though in slightly different context, the earth moved. The metal bars shifted and, slow motion, I fell through the brand new opening in the wall onto a grassy bank of plantings.

Well, shit. Twice in one week I'd ended up in the brush. Worse, when I got shakily to my feet, my ankle turned, gave out, and I half-fell, half-slid down the bank into a large puddle. My running shoes filled with cold, muddy water, and I was instantly soaked from the waist down.

An engine was still running on the other side of the wall, and seconds later a pair of headlights angled through the hole in the fence. Someone got out of the vehicle and stood back, just out of the light, facing in my direction. It was so unnerving, I scrambled out of the puddle, rolled under the sweeping fronds of a stand of areca palms and channeled invisibility.

It started to rain.

Crouching under a bunch of trees in wet underwear with snakes and rats and spiders lost its charm almost at once. My fear shifted to misery, then to anger and finally to disbelief. This was Seminole Beach, not Miami. I'd simply been sideswiped by a couple of boozing twenty year olds who got scared and backed up to see if they killed anybody. I crawled out from under scratchy palm fronds, mumbling several of my favorite four-letter words. By the time I limped to the hole in the wall, there was no one in sight to use them on.

But as I stepped through the wall into the alley, my anger

turned to caution. Someone had likely heard the crash and reported it. In this part of town, I might get picked up for trespassing in a gated community. I hustled away as quickly as possible, but walking was more difficult, and painful, than I anticipated.

When a pair of headlights swung onto the street, flashed on high and stayed behind me, I continued to hobble along in the rain, trying not to come down too hard on my left foot. The vehicle sounded loud, like the car in the alley, and it stayed with me as I moved along the sidewalk.

So much for liquored-up teenagers. I kept moving, looking for a house with lights, saving my ankle for one last rush up somebody's driveway to the front door. Just as I was ready to bolt, the headlights veered off and away from me, down a side street. They were replaced by those of a second car that pulled up directly beside me. A power window slid down.

"Are you having a problem? Can I help?"

I turned and looked into the twenty-five-year-old face of a Seminole Beach city police officer.

"I'm okay." I said, astonished that my voice sounded so matter of fact. "Tripped and fell while I was walking."

She was out of the car before I finished. "You did this," she was looking at my back, "falling? You'd better let me give you a ride. Where do you live?"

"Thirty-two East River Road." I limped over to the car, and she opened the passenger door for me.

"You think maybe you should see a doctor about that foot? I can take you by emergency."

"I'm fine, really. I'd just like to lie down in my own bed."

Neither of us said anything else during the three minutes it took to get home. I thanked her as I got out of the cruiser, but she stayed put until I unlocked the back door and went inside.

The kitchen lights were on, and Bear and Amy were at the worktable with a bottle of something red. Amy made me sit down, propped up my foot and poured me a glass of wine, while I explained why I was such a mess.

Bear picked leaves out of my wet hair. "What? You got a thing about rolling in the weeds?"

"Yeah, right." I gave him a vicious look. "I hate the outdoors. My idea of heaven is living over a coffee shop that sells international newspapers."

He grinned and disappeared upstairs, returning with an Ace bandage, which he wrapped from my heel to my knee.

Kenji wandered in to watch the wrapping process. "Do you know whole back of . . . jacket is torn . . . away?" There was a trace of awe in his voice.

"Somebody thinks you're on to something and wants you to quit," Bear said, pleased. "And whoever it is has a car. Father Mike must have one. Ms. Butler probably has several."

I drank an inch of wine. "She has a plane too. Maybe she flew to Seminole Beach and taxied down the alley after me."

Bear ignored all the words that didn't support his initial thought. "Good idea. She — or her foreman — could fly over from the ranch and back in ten minutes. They probably keep a car at the airport. But what is it you know? And what was the big deal about the oak hammock?"

"Oh, hell." In all the fuss of trying not to become road kill, I'd totally forgotten that, never mind my mind-blowing realization in the alley.

"I know how Stubb got in the church without setting off the alarm," I said to Bear, "and it wasn't through that tiny back window or a tunnel or by hiding in the church. It was easier than that. All he did . . ."

I reached across the table to Amy's computer, prepared to do show and tell, and got a surprise. The keyboard was so clean it gleamed. Somebody had been busy with a soapy sponge.

I felt the grin spread across my face. "And I also know who tried to run me down."

"Anybody seen Lee Lee?" Jesse said, as he shot through the swing door into the kitchen, rusty hair standing on end. "We were supposed to get pizza last night, but she didn't show. So she made it tonight, and now she's not in her room. Not only that — all her stuff's gone."

It took a minute before his words sunk in, then Bear got to his feet.

"I'll take a look upstairs," he said to Kenji. "You check the garage."

Kenji obeyed, but returned almost immediately.

"Jeep is missing," he said to Amy. "Did Lee Lee ask to borrow it?"

Amy shook her head no, as Bear re-entered the kitchen.

"Her bed's made," he reported, "and I think she's wiped all her fingerprints off everything."

Chapter 24

Amy was too wired to sleep after reporting her Jeep stolen. Instead, she mixed up a pitcher of white sangria and assembled ingredients for seafood paella. While she cut, chopped and sautéed, the rest of us had a debriefing session. I explained how Stubb had gotten into the church without tripping the alarm. Bear explained, at length, why Pete Beck was the obvious murderer, and Kenji explained why Bear was totally wrong. Jesse was so shocked by Lee Lee's treachery, he stayed in the kitchen, drinking beer, just like the old days. Maybe his reclusive period really was over. At any rate, we were all plastered by the time the paella hit the table, and it was after midnight before I crawled into bed.

Nevertheless, I was up and out of the house before eight the next morning. My left ankle was still swollen, in spite of six aspirins and an ice bag, but I didn't take time to coddle it. Twice during the night, I had snapped awake with the sure and certain knowledge that something bad was going to happen. And it wasn't just shellfish before bedtime. Somewhere out there, a nutso blonde with dark roots was planning something none of us was going to like.

I had a plan, but I didn't call Ms. Butler, who was first on my to-do list until I was several blocks from the house. Bear was probably still asleep, but if he wasn't, he'd insist on coming along. The errand I had in mind was strictly a one-woman proposition.

Candy Butler wasn't home. Her housekeeper-cook said she'd left for an early business meeting in West Palm and wouldn't be back until afternoon. That was an unexpected piece of luck; it meant a lot less lying and sneaking around.

I detoured downtown to Spike O's and ordered a double shot of espresso. The place was empty, except for the table of lawyers and businessmen who met every morning to discuss sports scores and the latest dumb thing the government was doing. I downed the coffee, took along a second one mixed with soy milk and headed west toward Lost River. Before tackling Candy Butler's hammock or pine cluster, or whatever the hell she wanted to call it, I wanted to ask Father Mike a couple of questions.

In spite of, or maybe because of the caffeine, my thoughts bounced all over the place. If Lee Lee was the hit-and-run driver, and it appeared she was, had she also taken a shot at me at the ranch? She'd mentioned horses on her family farm in Tennessee, and she probably knew how to use a rifle. But how had she managed to get on the Butler property when Bear and I couldn't? And how . . . Oh, wait. The night I met Pete for a drink, the bartender — Mindy something — had made a remark about blondes with roots. Lee Lee was certainly overdue for a touch-up. Maybe she hadn't been spending her time in Lost River checking out dirt; maybe she'd been out at the ranch checking out Pete Beck. But why shoot at me? She couldn't personally have killed Stubb Flanders. The night he died, she was never out of my sight, except when she went to the Porta-Potty.

Or did she? The truth was, she just *said* she was going to the little girl's room. I didn't really know where she'd been or what she'd been doing in the fifteen minutes she was away.

Lost River, once known as Rio Perdido, was basking in the sun, like the sleepy little town it had been before the discovery of magic earth. The smell of burning orange peel hung in the air, and a group of unemployed field-workers were squatting outside the Circle K. I drove down the main street past a line of huge old oak trees and found a place to park.

Father Mike's Mass must have ended bang-on schedule. He came down the steps of the church in one of his black, old fashioned-looking cassocks and stopped on the sidewalk when he saw me waiting for him.

"More questions, Mrs. Shaw?" His eyes were amused, if not smiling. "I understand you're not, er, helping Ms. Butler anymore."

"True, Father, but this isn't about Ms. Butler. I have a question about the burglar alarm."

"Ah." The amused look faded. "And what would that be?"

I was careful with my phrasing. "Do you actually set the alarm every night when you leave the church or is it sometimes left off?"

Nothing for a second. Then, "I put it on each and every evening at seven. Has someone suggested otherwise?"

"No." I looked him in the eye. "But around eleven thirty the night Stubb Flanders died, somebody opened one of the stained glass windows from the outside without tripping the alarm. That's why I'm asking."

"I can't imagine . . ." he began, then shrugged. "I follow the same procedure each day: check to be sure the windows and doors are locked and key in the four code numbers to set the alarm. If any of the windows were opened afterward, the siren should have gone off precisely two minutes later."

"Have you ever changed the code, Father? I mean, changed the numbers you picked when the system was installed?"

His chin got firmer. "Until now, there was never a reason."

"So, if anyone had known it to begin with, they'd know it now?"

"I suppose, but I hope you're not suggesting . . ."

"Does no one else have the code? Who opens up when you're sick or gone?"

His body seemed to thicken, even as he drew it up to full height. "I have never been too sick to fulfill my duties. And I'm never away."

I studied his face carefully. "Has the alarm ever gone off accidently or been cut or bypassed? Like in the last few weeks?"

"The police asked that question, as well, and the answer is no. We've had no trouble with it, and I'm careful to set and disarm it correctly."

We looked at each other for a long moment. I didn't know what he was thinking, but I was waiting for my B.S. indicator to screech: *Liar, liar, pants on fire.* Yeah, yeah, I know. Priests are supposed to tell the truth.

When nothing happened, I was actually relieved.

"Thank you, Father. I appreciate your time."

I limped away before he could ask any questions in return, pulled out my cell and unfolded the bar napkin Pete Beck had given me.

Pete answered on the first ring. "Yeah."

"Hi. It's Keegan Shaw. I know what you told me, but I had to come to Lost River anyway, and you said if I needed anything at all, I could call."

"Yeah?"

"I need something."

There was either a smile in his voice or I imagined it. "What can I do for you?"

"I need a favor. Can I come out to the ranch?"

There was a cautious silence. "You want to tell me what this is about?"

"Yes." I let my voice drop a quarter of an octave. "But not on the phone."

More silence. Then, "Come ahead. The gate's open. I'll be in the barn closest to the house."

On the way out to the ranch, I practiced what I was going to say, but when I limped through the open barn door, the script kind of got away from me. Pete was mixing oats and something else in a bucket, but he glanced up as I came in. His dark brows were almost straight over his eyes, and he looked like Jesse James about to knock over a bank. He exuded sex, in his black jeans and jacket — smoky, magnetic, you'll-be-sorry-later-but-ooh-baby sex. I wasn't sure how he did it, but as soon as I got in range, I wanted to rub his arm or shoulder or whatever part happened to be closest to me.

He leaned over the stall door to attach the bucket for the patiently waiting horse. The earthy, comforting smell of animals and loose hay reminded me of Sun Ridge Stables. I watched as Pete made the bucket fast and stroked the horse's neck with one palm. Then he turned, cocked his head at me and held out a hand.

I must have walked right into his arms. One minute I was standing there, minding my own business, planning what to say, the next I was attached solidly to the long, warm length of him, face pressed into his smooth, tanned neck, while he pulled me closer than I could technically get. I forgot about all the other women he was juggling and whether or not one of them was Lee Lee.

His mouth got warmer and harder, and so did everything else. *C'mon, Keegan*, I thought in a panic, Then I forgot about that too, as he swung me off my feet and carried me toward an empty stall.

"Wait." The part of my brain that still worked apparently wasn't willing to do it in a damned barn. Well, maybe.

"Wait," I said louder, and added those five little words all men hate to hear, "We need to talk first."

Sometime later, Pete Beck leaned against the stall door and regarded me, unsmiling.

"Not a good idea," he said, almost under his breath. He was one hundred percent against either of us riding out to the hammock, and he was clearly skeptical when I said I'd lost my grandmother's antique wristwatch during the storm.

But after several more minutes of intimate discussion, he agreed to give me half an hour to search for my much-loved heirloom. Then he saddled the horse I'd ridden before and rode silently beside me in the direction I wanted to go.

Pete looked unsettled as well as irritable, but I was giving myself credit for remembering I had a plan at all. The aftereffects of a minor earthquake take time to dissipate.

Chapter 25

It was colder outside than I had realized, maybe the high sixties, but the sun was dazzling. Everything in Florida, even scrub and swamp, looks beautiful with sunshine spilling over it.

My horse was a little jittery, probably a reaction to the last time I took him for a ride. He shied twice, once when birds flew up out of a stand of palmettos and again when a rabbit hopped backward into our path. Which seemed odd; he must have seen rabbits before. Maybe he was suffering from post-traumatic stress.

Due to Bear's expert bandaging, my ankle barely hurt, and it took no time at all to reach the place that had scared me into spasms two evenings before. My strategy was simple to the point of non-existent: I intended to stay safely in the saddle while I tried to see what there was about a bunch of trees that would make somebody hack a trail through them and then shoot at me to keep me away. I thought I knew, but my bright idea might be a total waste of time. Like Bear's trip to the stables.

However, the closer we got, the more I realized I needed a couple of backup ideas. I could poke around that clump of trees for hours without stumbling across anything important. Plus, I wasn't sure how long Pete would let me look for my mythical watch before calling a halt.

Ms. Butler's foreman was with me physically, but that didn't mean he was actively helping. After some initial floundering, I found the path somebody had chopped into the undergrowth and approached the opening. Now what? I wasn't worried about being shot at again, not in bright sunlight and not with Pete along. Bear might suspect Pete of being the bad guy in the story, but I never had. Still, the place was more than borderline creepy, even in sunny daylight.

I was gathering up enough nerve to enter the thicket, when Pete said, "You're not going in there . . . ?" Then his expression changed, and he stared past me. My horse skittered a little and backed away from the hand-cut trail.

Another rider had appeared on the path, meandering out of the overgrowth to meet us. The sun backlit a man and horse as they left the shadows, and I started to smile.

He wore the same plaid shirt, the same baseball cap, the same air of serenity, but today there was no calf or Lone Ranger mask. Obviously, living rough in a Florida hammock beat the hell out of drinking yourself to death in a trailer park.

Pete, who managed to look surprised and ticked off at the same time, had stopped his horse several yards back, but I kept going until I got within a few feet of Bobby McCleod. Bobby McCleod, alias Porky Joe. Bobby McCleod, who called himself

Red the day Bear and I cornered him in the trailer.

I was surprised how happy I was to see him. We traded tentative smiles as we faced each other, and the sense of calm he radiated could have solved the problems of me, my skittish horse and most of the free world.

"You gave me honey that day," he said, glancing at the foreman. "How'd you find me?"

"Pete didn't tell me," I assured him. "I guessed. One of your mother's mares had been taken from the barn, and it finally hit me that a pine cluster would be a dandy place to hide out on a horse. Except you'd have to chop a trail into it to avoid scratching up its legs." I held up a palm. "I didn't know why you'd do that, but you were brought up on this ranch, and you'd gone missing. So I took a chance."

Bobby pointed a finger at the foreman and pulled an imaginary trigger. "My mother know?"

Pete lifted his chin in acknowledgment. "Saw you the night it stormed, but she thought you moved to another part of the pasture. Said to leave you awhile, let you get your head straightened out."

"Good old mom."A smile tugged at the corner of Bobby's mouth. "I did move, but I came back. It always felt better here."

After that, none of us spoke for awhile. The day was warming up fast, and the smell of new-cut grass drifted in from a nearby field. It was so still, so peaceful, I could have sat there all day and ditched the questions I'd been so anxious to ask. In fact, I considered it, but eventually, my need to know beat out my need for peace.

When I did say something, it felt like the easiest thing in the world. "Why did you hit Stubb?"

"Not because of my brother." An uneasy look flitted across

Bobby's face. "He couldn't understand. After everything that had happened to Scott, to me, all those years of nothing good, Stubb didn't learn anything. Just went on doing what he did best . . . wrecking things."

"Did you know he was going to be at the church that night?"

"No. I couldn't believe it when I heard he was in my town. But I should have known. It was my fault, really. Another mistake. I didn't think it through."

He leaned back on the horse and drew up his knees. "My buddies and I used to hang in that church yard, have a drink or two, you know? And when I saw Stubb out back that night, I knew he was up to no good. Everybody in town knew he was threatening Father Mike about something that happened up north."

He looked out across the pasture. "Carlos and Red got wasted right away, but I rationed myself and watched. And sure enough, after awhile, Stubb slipped around to the side door. He looked over at the table and shrugged us off as a useless bunch of drunks. You could see it on his face. Then he opened the door and went inside. I waited for the alarm to go off, for all hell to break loose, but nothing happened. So I followed him."

"You couldn't have." I protested. "I was out front, watching you guys all night. I'd have seen you"

Bobby shrugged. "It took about six seconds to walk to that door, and you never looked my way. My mother was asking you a lot of questions."

She had been. I frowned. "Keeping me occupied, on purpose?"

"I don't think so. Probably didn't know it was me. But Luane saw me when she went around back. She'd have made sure you didn't look up. She's always got my back."

"Luane." I gave him a look. "Luane/Lee Lee who tried to run me down last night?"

He seemed surprised. "Did she? Probably trying to scare you off. She said you were wicked smart, and if anybody could figure out what happened to Stubb, it would be you."

I let that go. "What happened when you got in the church?"

"Stubb was already in the dirt room, setting up his tripod. He didn't recognize me until I called him by name. Took a long, hard look at me and started laughing.

"When I asked how he got in without setting off the alarm, he acted like it was a compliment. He said, 'Well, Bobby, I couldn't have if the cleaning girl wasn't so bloody lazy. The key pad had years of oily fingerprints daubed around the same four buttons — one, two, three, four. I spent a couple hours working out all the possible number combinations and came up with twenty-four. Every time I came to the church I tried some to see if they worked and one day they did. And you know what the code was? One, two, three, four. The same fucking number it had when it came from the factory. They're thick as two planks out here."

I smiled to myself. My brainstorm in the alley had been correct.

"He wouldn't shut up about how smart he was." Bobby was going on, his face set in unhappy lines. "He said, 'I paid the girl to clean the alarm pad, then realized she might mention it, so I made her clean the hallway and the door and the window in the back room. She wasn't clever enough to suss out what really mattered. And then I put a piece of tape over the lock on the side door before I left. It stayed like that for two days, and nobody even noticed. What a bunch of dip-sticks."

Ms. Butler's son shifted his position on the horse, and his

voice hardened. "He was so shot with his own program, attaching his camera to the tripod and smirking. He said, 'I'm putting a stop to the ignorant idea that this place can cure anything at all. I'm waiting right here, camera ready, until the cretin who brings in the famous earth sneaks in with more of same. And then everybody will know what a joke it is. Rubbing dirt on yourself. Jesus Christ.' "

"Then he turned his back on me. Like I didn't matter. My life wasn't worth much, and Scott's was over, and all he wanted to do was make people look stupid. I grabbed up the tripod and swung it at him."

Bobby rocked forward over the neck of his horse and the animal made a comforting whicker. When he spoke again, the words were so soft, I had to lean forward to hear.

"He didn't get up, and I thought he was playing possum so I wouldn't hit him again. That's the Stubb I knew. Wait 'til you're gone and then call the police. So I took the edge of my shirt and wiped my prints off the tripod and put his fingers all over it. I stood there for the longest time, waiting for him to come around. But he didn't move, and there was blood all over his face, and I kind of panicked. I reset the alarm with the numbers he said: one, two, three, four — with my knuckles so he couldn't prove I'd been there — took the tape off the door latch and closed it, and ran back to the picnic table. None of you were even looking my way."

He breathed out a sigh into the horse's mane. "My jacket was there, and I put it on because my shirt was all messed up. Carlos and Red were still sacked out on the table, and I put my head down and waited, freezing to death, to see if Stubb came out." He raised his head and said in a matter-of-fact voice, "You know he never did."

The sun went under a cloud, and I felt a shudder move through me. After awhile, I said, "Where does Lee Lee come in?"

He rubbed his hand along the horse's neck. "We stayed in touch after high school. Couple years ago, I looked her up in Miami. When I decided to come up here, I didn't tell her, just sent a postcard a few months later. She came up to track me down and hung around the church, but I wasn't using my own name. I didn't want my mother to know I was in town."

"Then why come back here?"

He laughed out loud. "For the cure, of course. St. Jude's miraculous cure. I could get sober, but I couldn't stay sober. It was kind of my last shot. As soon as Lee Lee saw the postcard, she knew what was up."

"From a postcard?"

"I was drunk when I sent it." He looked sheepish. "It was a picture of St. Jude's."

I grinned at him. "Not like you wanted to be found. It's a wonder you didn't send Stubb one too."

"How'd you know?"

I nearly fell off my horse. "I was joking. You honestly sent him a card?"

"Well, a brochure of St. Jude's. I thought . . . I knew where he was, see. A photographer I used to know had seen him in New York, trying to get a job. He gave me Stubb's card and said I should take out a contract on him. I think . . . I don't know. I was drunk. I think I was trying to forgive him . . ."

"But instead, he came here to spoil what peace you'd found."

Bobby shrugged.

"But why shoot Carlos? Or was that Luane?"

His head was moving back and forth. "Not us. Don't know who that was. Or why."

I looked in his eyes and saw he believed it.

"So, what now? Your mother seems prepared to take the blame for you."

"Not this time. I'll send a letter. Explain later." He moved awkwardly on the horse's back and his voice sounded suddenly young. ". . . my dog wasn't doing anything wrong that day. He was just running with me, and that asshole picked up his rifle and shot him. I ran at him and knocked him down and grabbed the gun. When the sheriff came, there was my stepfather, dead with the dog's body. I didn't even remember shooting him.

"My mother told the deputies she shot the dog because it was chasing the horses. Then she sent Scott and me away, and I got hypnotized every day for a month, and after awhile, I knew I'd done it, but I didn't remember much about it."

I stared at Bobby McCleod, sitting on his horse, no reins, no saddle, just hanging there, as if it was the most natural thing in the world. Out here, his face was nearly wrinkle-free, and his eyes had lost the deep sadness of his senior picture.

I leaned toward him. "Which one are you, really?"

"What?" The aura of serenity dimmed a little.

"Are you Bobby or are you really Scott?"

He blinked at me. "Scott . . . Scott died, didn't he? I must be Bobby."

I darted a glance at Pete, who was sitting straight up in the saddle, eyes narrowed to slits. He looked like he might shoot me any second.

"Thanks for talking to me," I said to the boy — the man — on the horse. "Nobody will hear about this meeting from me. And I'm sorry about Stubb Flanders . . . what he did."

"Here," his hand went in his pocket and came out with a cell phone, "this is his. I took it so he couldn't call the police after I left. Whatever you decide to do with it is okay." His smile was as warm as a blessing. "I've been wanting to talk to somebody neutral about it." He nudged his horse around with his knees, eyes on the phone in my hand, "We were nothing alike, Stubb and me, not really. But we both went out to the jungle. And we're both drunks."

Chapter 26

Pete made it absolutely clear, on the ride back to the barn, that he was interested in nothing from me, either now or at any time in the future. When I got off my horse, I handed over the reins and spoke to his averted face.

"I know you're pissed at me, but I won't forget that you came and got me out of that thicket when I was scared to death. Or how warm you were riding back. Or . . . anything else."

He walked the two horses back toward the barn as if I didn't exist.

Apparently, he reported my presence at the ranch to Candy Butler. Somebody did, because that evening she left several messages on my cell phone. All were abrupt. The first two asked me to call her, the last ones stopped just short of "Call me or die."

When I did phone the following day, she ordered me out to the ranch.

"Sorry." I held the cell away from my ear while she added -ing to a lot of four-letter words, but after a couple of minutes, I got tired of it. It wasn't like she needed the practice.

"You can come here if you want to talk to me," I interrupted. "Not to the house, downtown at the River Walk. I'll be there at two o'clock."

I figured it was fifty-fifty whether she'd actually turn up, but she did, twenty-two fashionable minutes late. I was sitting on one of the stone benches, looking out at the wide river, when I heard her cowboy boots clattering down the wooden steps leading to the walk. It was another perfect beach day, but I doubt Ms. Butler noticed. She had apparently been dipped, head to toe, in vitriolic acid. She radiated hostility.

"You stupid . . . bitch." She came to a stop directly in front of me. "Who the fuck do you think you are? Coming on my property, lying to my foreman, cross-examining my son . . ."

She wasn't quite spitting in my face, but the effect was the same, and it drew apprehensive looks from a couple of people jogging by.

I stood up and put some space between us. Lately, it seemed I was attracting people who got off on swearing at me in public. Maybe I was lacking in self-esteem.

"I'm the person whose dossier you're going to destroy as soon as you get home," I said in an even voice. "You missed a lot of stuff the first time: speeding tickets, criminal record, birthmarks, unsavory habits. It stops now. And the same goes for any information you've gathered on my friends or the people living in my house."

It took her by surprise, I think. She was used to knocking

people flat in one furious onslaught, not dealing with back talk.

"I paid you good money . . ."

"It came this morning." I pulled the cashier's check out of my pocket and held it out. "I told you not to. I don't take money from people who try to shoot me."

She snatched the check out of my hand, folded it in half and shoved it down one boot. Classy. The venomous look in her eyes was now edged with wariness.

"What do you want, then?"

"Not Pete."

The eyes didn't even blink. "Pete never could keep it in his pants. But I guess you know that by now."

I gave what I hoped was an irritating shrug. "Not my problem."

"Hmmph. Well, don't get your hopes up; he's not going anywhere."

"Really? He's twenty years younger than you . . ."

"He'll never leave the ranch," she blurted out. "It all goes to him."

I let the surprise show on my face. "What about Bobby?"

"Pete'll look after him. Somebody'll have to." She shrugged. "So, if it's not money, what do you want?"

"For starters, I want to know why you shot at me."

"Don't waste my time."

"You asked. That's what I want."

Her head turned toward the river for a few seconds, then swung back around. For the first time, I noticed dark gray smudging around her eyes.

"You already talked to my kid, so I guess it doesn't matter. I saw him darting in and out of the trees on my missing mare about the time you rode up to the hammock. I didn't want you to find out he was hiding in there, so I provided some distraction. No big deal."

"Not to you, apparently. You honestly didn't know he was hiding on the ranch?"

"I didn't even know he was in town. But he used to run away from his stepfather, him and Scott both. Hide out there for hours with his dog. Wear a black mask, pretend to shoot Indians. He carried his dog across the front of his saddle like a calf. He was always happier out there than anywhere else."

"What about Carlos? The onion picker. Did you provide some distraction for him too?"

Her shoulder lifted a fraction of an inch. "He followed Bobby to the ranch. Saw him take the mare out of the stable. After the storm, when you left in such a hurry, he rode up on his bicycle, soaking wet, and asked for money. Bobby had been talking when he was drunk, and that spick figured out who he really was."

"Isn't that blackmail? Why not just report him to the Sheriff?"

"First off, I don't report anything to the sheriff and, second, they woulda known Bobby was in the churchyard that night. He'd have been in a cell in three seconds flat."

"So you shot the poor bastard instead of paying him off?"

"I never said that." Her chin jerked up, and her lip line thinned. "He had a lot of enemies. People like him get shot sooner or later. And Bobby was overdue for some justice. There's got to be some for people so damaged they can't get it themselves."

"You know Bobby killed Stubb, though, right?"

For a second, she didn't move. "I haven't talked to him," she said finally. "He's not at the hammock anymore."

I felt my eyes widen, though I wasn't sure why. You can't live in a hammock forever. Not even if you're the Lone Ranger.

"The police never called you to come to Palm Beach and identify him, did they? You lied about that too."

Another shoulder shrug. "Just trying to keep him out of it."

"You know where Bobby is now?"

Her black, curly head made a negative motion, and her voice was harsh. "The mare was back in her stall early this morning. I sent Pete out to look, but there wasn't any sign of him."

I'd have felt sorry for her, if it hadn't been wasted emotion. "Why didn't you ever get him some help?" I said, echoing his eighth-grade teacher. "Like the first time, when he killed his stepfather?"

She gaped at me. "He told you that?"

"He said his stepfather shot his dog."

She took a breath that seemed to suck up all the air around her. "The boys were supposed to be helping with the fence, and Bobby lost a tool or something, hell I don't know what. Gil started beating on him. It wasn't the first time. The dog jumped on both of them, and Gil shot the dog. Bobby went crazy and grabbed the gun."

"And you let people think you'd done it?"

She drew her shoulders up. "I always tried to protect my boys. Bobby was too sensitive, and Scott was . . . well, careless, kind of wild."

"And then they went to Bolivia, and one of them got killed, and the other one never got over it. Which one did I see in the hammock? Bobby or Scott? Are you sure Bobby's actually the one who shot his stepfather."

"The truth?" Her gaze shifted to her left boot. "I don't know any more."

I stared at her for a long second, then turned away.

'We're not done here," Her voice hardened.

"Yeah, we are."

"But — what are you going to do about all this?"

"Nothing. As long as I don't see or hear from you anymore."

She shifted her boots on the boardwalk. "I'd be happier if you'd take back the check."

I shook my head. "Nope."

"So, what did you do?" Her mouth twisted in a half-smile. "Write a letter and ask a friend to keep it, in case something happened to you?"

"Is that what the people who deal with you usually do?"

Her eyes got that flat look again, and I hoped she hadn't come armed.

"Let's be clear about this. I stay away from you — and yours — and you don't go to the sheriff with any crazy ideas you have about me or my son. Is that it?"

"That's it." I turned to go, then hesitated as a thought slipped into my head. "By the way, did you ever date a car dealer from Seminole Beach? One who claimed he'd seen your first husband in Mexico, licking another guy's face?"

Her mouth opened, closed, opened again and clamped shut.

Instead of taking the stairs to the street, I took the path that wound around in front of City Hall. It was stupid, but I didn't want to go back the same way she'd come. Some of that deadly Candy Butler energy might still be hanging in the air.

"You were kind of hard on her, weren't you?"

The voice came from behind a tall hedge of pink flowering trees, but it was a voice I knew.

"Where were you?" I said, as Bear joined me on the path.

"Stretched out behind the sedge grass above the bench. I

repeat, you were kind of hard on her. She's lost both sons now, probably. All she did was try to protect them. Where's your womanly compassion?"

"I don't waste it on treacherous people. She's standing down there right now, trying to figure out how to get even with me."

"You don't think you're exaggerating a little?"

"No. It's possible Bobby shot his stepfather, and it haunted him the rest of his life. It's more likely she took the gun out of his hand and killed Gil herself."

Bear looked disbelieving. "And let the kid think he did it?"

"Well, she sent him away. I think she did a double-double. The only thing she told me, that I believe absolutely, is that she's claustrophobic. She was almost sweating when she said the word, jerking her chair around and gasping for air. I think she pretended she shot her husband in a way that made the detectives sure the kid did it. I don't know if Bobby couldn't remember what happened or if she just told him he did it until he believed her. She was betting the cops wouldn't charge him, and she thought he'd forget all about it, after awhile. That's what she'd have done." I shrugged "Of course, there's a chance Scott did it and Bobby took the blame, but I think it was her."

"I smell another intuitive leap." Bear grunted. "It could still be old Pete, the foreman. He was working on the ranch at the time, and he's got a lot invested in his job. He's practically family: flies the plane whenever he wants, drives her cars whenever he wants." He gave me a sideways look. "Fools around whenever he wants, probably."

I nodded. "True. He also inherits the ranch when she dies."

"Shit, you're kidding. I didn't hear that part. Why do things like that never happen to me?"

"Because you have too much character to get involved with a woman who probably offed two husbands?"

"Two!"

"Well, they never found the body of the interior decorator. If you take away the Mexico story, which she most likely planted, you just have a guy who hasn't been seen since they found a pile of his clothes out at the locks. What do you think?"

"She's some piece of work, huh." Bear shook his head. "Maybe you better hire a bodyguard for awhile. By the way, Amy's Jeep turned up. One whole side's mashed in, and the police have it, but she'll get it back, eventually."

"Where was it?"

"The bus station."

"Really. How unimaginative of good old Lee Lee."

Chapter 27

A full week passed without the sheriff's department releasing Stubb's body. Word was, they were searching for next of kin or, failing that, somebody legally authorized to take charge. It didn't seem to be a speedy process.

Maggie was upset about the situation but calmer than I expected. That was probably due to Bear, who upped her run to twice a day and signed her up for survivor yoga in the park. It's called survivor yoga because it begins at dawn, and if the fertilizer the city puts on the grass doesn't finish you — or the flying and crawling bugs — then the instructor, a Desert Storm vet, probably will.

Bear also made her sit down one night and list the dates and amount of hours she'd actually spent in Stubb's company over the last fifteen years. I think the real number was a shock.

Basing the premier tragedy of your life on a couple of years of actual contact is hard to justify. She assimilated the new information better than I hoped, and that was probably due to the white cat whose name was now Elmer. It had filled out a little from regular feeding, and it followed Maggie around like a dog.

She was astonishingly calm when she reported her final conversation with the coroner's office.

"A friend can't claim the body in this county, and it's too expensive to cremate unclaimed bodies, so I can't even scatter Stubb's ashes. They'll bury him in a potter's field." She shook her head. "On the other hand, Stubb might like to stay in one place, by way of a change. Instead of always being on the run."

"Maybe," I agreed, "still, he did have a sense of humor. When he wasn't drinking or pissed off. Maybe he'd prefer something a little more iconic for his . . . last act."

"I remember that tone of voice, Keegan." Maggie regarded me with suspicion. "What, precisely, did you have in mind?"

I told her.

A week later, Maggie and Bear and I drove out to Lost River, parked a few blocks from St. Jude's and made our way to the empty field behind the church. We were screened by trees and bushes, and we didn't plan to stay long enough to attract either attention or trouble.

Bear was carrying a folding shovel he said he'd got in the Marines, but it was the first I'd heard about him being in the service. He dug a fairly deep hole at the edge of the pile of earth used to replenish the dirt room, and we took turns burying our memories of Stubb Flanders.

I'd retrieved the pink gun, the one Stubb had used to shoot out my car window, from Jesse's herb garden, along with his flask. I went first, placing both items in the bottom of the hole, but I couldn't think of any suitable accompanying words. "Take that, idiot boy," didn't seem like the right tone.

Bear held up Stubb's cell phone, the one Bobby McCleod had appropriated the night of the murder, the one Maggie had given Stubb before he came to Florida. "You sure about burying this? It might have calls on it the deputies want to check."

"If we give it to them, they'll start looking for Maggie. If we wait a couple of days, I think they'll hear from Bobby, and the phone will be a non-issue. There's no evidence on it anyway. Bobby only made two calls on it — both to Lee Lee Lee, and she never said where she was taking him, only where she was picking him up."

"Your call." Bear tossed the cell phone on top of the flask without any words of farewell.

Maggie went last, and she took her time. The Ziploc bag of St. Jude's magic earth came out of her purse, along with a CD player she'd borrowed from Amy. She poured the earth into the hole in a steady stream, then turned on the CD player.

Music blared out, and she hastily adjusted the volume.

"It's Meatloaf," she said, briefly, "Two Out of Three Ain't Bad," Stubb's favorite song. She removed the CD and tossed it in the hole.

I've heard a lot of songs played at funerals, most notably "Hello, Dolly," but never one about a guy who said he wanted a girl, needed her, but insisted there was no way he was ever going to love her. Hence, the two out of three ain't bad. It struck me funny to the point of hysteria; I couldn't help it. I turned away so Maggie didn't see, and there was Father Mike, emerging from the trees at the back of the church, walking slowly across the field in our direction.

That sobered me up fast. After all, we were trespassing in a pretty big way.

Father Mike looked into the hole Bear had dug and appeared to be memorizing the items in it.

"Uh, Father," I was almost stuttering, "I'm really sorry. We should have, uh . . ."

He raised a palm. "Nothing wrong with a bit of closure. I would like to add something, if there are no objections."

When nobody said anything, he leaned down, picked up a handful of earth and dropped it into the hole. His accent became more pronounced.

"We have left undone those things which we ought to have done; and we have done those things which we ought not to have done."

He stood silently, letting the familiar words from the *Book of Common Prayer* hang in the air before reaching for another handful of soil.

"Earth to earth, ashes to ashes, dust to dust; in the sure and certain hope of the resurrection into eternal life."

I shivered. We might have been standing on a bleak Irish hillside in an ice storm instead of in balmy inland Florida.

In the silence that followed, I was rooted to that isolated section of field, conscious of how small and enclosed life could get if you weren't careful. Of how easy it is to be crowded-in by too many memories. I was also aware of Maggie, standing next to me, waiting for some kind of answer, or at least some clarity.

But Stubb was as elusive here as he was in life, his existence marked by a cell phone that belonged to somebody else, a gun that probably did too, a flask, a CD expressing his position on love, and healing dirt he hadn't believed in.

Tears ran down Maggie's face, but she let them fall without wiping them away, and she didn't look guilty or devastated. More like she'd been let out on parole and didn't know what to do about it.

After awhile, Bear picked up his shovel and filled in the hole. He smoothed it across the top, then put an arm around Maggie and walked her back in the direction of the car.

Father Mike and I stood together, looking at the smoothed-over spot. Eventually, I began to feel better, less sorry for the world and all of us in it.

"Thank you, Father. I don't know if that was for Stubb or Maggie, but . . ."

"For both. Also for me." He raised his head and looked me in the eye. "There's something I'd like to tell you in Mr. Flanders' presence. The day this miracle business began, I walked by the door to the earth room. Andreas' stepfather had carried some broken paving outside, and the boy was playing in the dirt that was under it. Making noises. I spoke from the doorway, more on a whim than anything else.

"God is everywhere, Andreas," I said in my full priest's voice, "even in the earth. The earth will help you speak." And then I walked on. The next thing I knew, the miracle story was all over town, and I was too mortified to explain. I allowed it to grow, to become a phenomenon, by not telling the truth of the matter, immediately. When I found Mr. Flanders' body, I was certain he'd been killed because of my arrogance, no matter who or what the instrument."

I looked from the smoothed-over hole to the field around us. Except for the imported mound of dirt, it must have looked exactly the same for hundreds of years. Maybe thousands. Must be a message there somewhere.

"Irish guilt is a fine thing, Father," I said finally. "If you'd told the truth, they'd still have called it a miracle."

"Possibly." His voice was without expression. "But the boy thought I was God."

A couple of days later, Maggie and I took a thermos of coffee down to the seawall and sat by the river. I had retrieved my suitcase of memories from under the bed, and for a couple of hours we pawed through photos, letters, newspaper clippings and odds and ends, discussing where we'd been and where we might be headed. It was easy, effortless talk, like the old days, when we worked together. When Stubb's name came up, and it did, it seemed more a part of those days than it did of the present.

By the time we'd run out of coffee and meaningful words, the sun was gone, and the thick cloud cover made it look like snow might fall any moment.

"I probably should be getting back to New York," Maggie said after a long, comfortable silence. The white cat was curled in her lap, paws covering its nose.

"You don't have to."

"I know." She sighed, and it turned into a yawn. "But in my family, you don't indulge shocks to the system, you just get on with it. Hard work, the answer to all the world's ills." Her mouth twisted a little. "I expect I can get my job back if I ask nicely. Now that Stubb is no longer part of the picture."

"You can stay here as long as you want. Bear regards you as a great success. Nothing he loves better than wallowing in credit."

"He deserves to. He literally dragged me out of the trench I'd dug for myself. I've never had a very addictive personality," she stopped, and her face got pink, "except when it came to Stubb, obviously, but I'd got so I was pouring down drinks, just to get through the day."

"Maybe you were cured by St. Jude's magic earth," I said. "You spent a long time in that room. Of course, so did Lee Lee. She said she was waiting for voices — messages — but that was another one of her stories. I don't think she has a spiritual bone in her body; she just wanted to save Bobby."

"Speaking of which," Maggie leaned down and rubbed the cat's ears, "You know me. You know I'm not good at emotional stuff, but I want you know . . ." She raised her head and looked me in the eye. "Because of you, I got my life back, Keegan. I realize it made a lot of trouble for you, and if I could do something to make amends, I would. But I can't think of anything meaningful enough. We'll just have to leave it that I owe you."

I smiled at her and shook my head. "I could have made that same speech to you several years ago. We're even now." I leaned over the suitcase, pushed aside a cigarette lighter from the KOKO Club, a wonderfully sleazy London rock club from the Nineties, and pulled a photograph out of the pile. It was a picture of me at about twenty-six, taken with Rob, who was still the best looking guy I'd ever dated.

"Without you," I said to Maggie, waving the photograph, "I'd have lost my career, probably my sanity and might even now be occupying an English prison. I've never forgotten you swore blind — to a magistrate — that I was in Wales with you the weekend Rob's wife claimed I tried to kill her."

Maggie flipped red hair behind one ear. "She was a total nutter. And besides, I warned you not to get mixed up with the boss. Rule Number One, no married men, and Number Two, absolutely never your own editor."

"So you did." I dropped the photograph back in the case and picked up an old, beaten-up periodical with Maggie's by-line on the cover.

"Concepts Magazine. And poor Rob, with a wife so jealous she stabbed herself in the side, twice. I was crazy about him you know. For awhile, I didn't think I'd ever get over it. And then I met Jack. And you know how beautifully that turned out." I hesitated, "Speaking of which . . ."

A smile touched her lips. "I know. The last thing I want is to end up with another . . . mistake. I'll have to get my head straight, see someone for awhile." She made a face. "You know how I detest people with *issues* who have to go to therapy . . ."

Her attention shifted back to the suitcase. "So, what's the plan for your old karma? Toss it? Bury it? Or stick it back under the bed?"

"Oh, a fire I think. A nice, purifying fire."

"Knock yourself out." Maggie reached in the suitcase and handed me the KOKO's cigarette lighter.

It had been living in the past too, obviously, because it didn't work anymore.

Chapter 28

Detective Christensen showed up at the house the following day to see if we'd heard anything from Lee Lee, alias Luane Keiner.

I told him no, but he stuck around for awhile anyway.

"No idea where in Miami she lived?"

"She never said."

"She stayed here a week, and you don't know her address or phone number or anything about her? Hell of a way to run a business."

"It isn't a business, and she wasn't paying rent. She was a guest for four days. I didn't even know her last name until you told me. Didn't you get her address when you talked to her?"

"Yeah." He shook his head in disgust. "She hasn't been around there for weeks."

From the tone of his questions, I was guessing Bobby had sent the department the letter he promised and taken responsibility for Stubb's death. Hopefully, he hadn't sent it on motel stationary from wherever he was holed up. Being on the lam with Lee Lee was probably the smartest thing he'd done lately.

I felt a tiny twinge of guilt about burying Stubb's cell phone, but it wouldn't have helped them find Bobby anyway. Besides, I thought he deserved some justice too.

"All I know is Lee Lee turned up at St. Jude's the same night I did," I said to Christensen, "and she didn't have any place to stay, so I let her come here. She was the perfect houseguest. Went out to see the magic dirt for several days and then, apparently, headed home."

I didn't mention she'd tried to run me down in the process, which was big of me; I was still annoyed about it.

The detective looked skeptical. "She never mentioned where she was going or what she did for a living?"

"No, but you could ask Jesse. He spent a lot of time with her."

"He the one on the porch with all the pots?"

"That's him."

Christensen went out to the front porch, but I doubted he'd get much information from Jesse. Come to think of it, I didn't even know where Jesse came from. Amy probably knew. She keeps track of stuff like that.

There was a knock on the back door, and I went to see who it was. The mailman was standing on the sidewalk with a registered letter. He handed me a clipboard to sign. "You have a nice day, now."

There was no return address. I ripped open the envelope, which had been mailed in Cordele, Georgia and took out a folded sheet of notebook paper.

Dear Keegan,

Bobby said he talked to you, but I just wanted to say I'm sorry. I'd been hanging around St. Jude's day and night, figuring he'd show up sooner or later, when I ran into you guys. And I wasn't lying about being out of money. That's why I was camped out in front of the church.

When I spotted Bobby in the church yard that night, I said I was going around to talk to that Stubb guy, but I really went to see what Bobby was up to. But I couldn't tell, so I just kept quiet and watched. When they found the body, I couldn't believe it. Bobby called me on that Stubb's phone and said what he'd done, and I told him to sit tight, but before I could figure something out, you and Bear found him at the trailer, and he panicked and went to hide at the ranch.

I knew I made a mistake that day in the kitchen, when I started babbling about Amy's dirty computer keys. Bobby told me how Stubb got in the church without setting off the alarm, and I guess it was really on my mind. I handed you the clue, just like that, and I could see you were going to figure it out before long. So, I talked real loud and ran upstairs and dialed the kitchen phone to maybe knock it out of your head. And when you went out for a walk, I cleaned off the computer keys and borrowed Amy's Jeep and followed you.

I really am sorry about that part. I wasn't trying to run you down, just — you know — scare you so you'd stop doing any more investigating. Anyway, it all turned out okay. Bobby thinks you're the best.

Thanks for giving me a place to stay. The food was great, and I really liked all of you. Have a happy life and try to forgive me, if you can.

Love,
Lee Lee

P.S. Tell Kenji I'm sorry I took his two photographs. That was dumb. Should have known he'd just make more.

I folded the piece of paper up into a tight little package and decided it was one more thing to burn. In spite of what Bobby thought, I had a feeling flaky old Lee Lee was every bit as ruthless as Candy Butler. Especially when it came to something she wanted. After all, she'd packed up everything and removed her fingerprints *before* she'd followed me in the Jeep.

Of course, I might be wrong; only Lee Lee knew for sure. And I didn't know if she and Bobby McCleod had actually boarded a Greyhound bus for parts unknown, or merely used it as a blind. But I'd have bet every last cent that if Christensen wanted to find them, he should look up in Northern Tennessee for a dark haired girl (who'd once been blonde) and a boyfriend who shouted, "Hi Ho Silver!"

Maggie went back to New York a couple of weeks later, carrying Elmer in a special bag on the plane. That's how life works for cats. One minute you're living hungry in a horse barn, the next you're in a condo on the lower East side.

Bear stuck close to me for a week after that. He was afraid Ms. Butler might try to get even with me for screwing up her life.

At one point, I asked him why he'd been worried about the police investigation.

"Some big secret in your life you don't want anyone finding out?"

He shrugged me off. "Hey, you know Florida, the last frontier. Everybody here's on the run from something or somebody."

"You're not going to tell me, are you?"

"Nope."

Bear went back upstairs to do whatever he does up there, and I talked Amy out of one of her salted caramel lattes, which is always a mistake, because they're a thousand calories each, and I suck them down way too fast.

"What's the deal with Bear" I said to her. "Why was he so concerned about being investigated?"

She leaned against the kitchen counter and studied me. "Can you keep a secret? A big one?"

When I nodded, she said in a low voice, "He isn't really from out West, like he pretends. Bear was raised in New Jersey by a nutso mother. He keeps a low profile because he's always afraid she'll track him down and ask for money."

"He doesn't have any."

"Well, actually, he does. In spite of appearances, Bear is a trust fund baby — thanks to his paternal grandmother. Since he was sixteen."

At my look of astonishment, Amy giggled. "Explains a lot, doesn't it?"

Tom Roddler called much later that evening, when I was up in the mezzanine, in bed, watching *NCIS* reruns. I saw his name on the screen, but I muted Leroy Jethro Gibbs and reminded myself that Tom might always be Tom, but I didn't have to spend my life being pissed off at him.

"I understand everything got solved," he said, without preamble.

"I think so. The police have pretty much stopped coming around."

"I heard they're looking for some guy who used to live in Lost River. Listen," Tom's voice was uncharacteristically sober. "I also heard how much trouble you've had with Candy Butler. This is the second time I've landed you in shit." He paused. "I promise it won't happen again."

I was so surprised, I kept quiet. It was the first time he'd ever promised me anything.

"I suppose the English rocker boyfriend is still in the picture?" he said, after a moment.

"He's coming here for Christmas."

He let out a long, slow breath. "Just don't count me out, okay? Not yet."

Postscript

Bear quit playing bodyguard last Tuesday, when they found Candy Butler dead from a gunshot in the same hammock her son had used for a hideout. The sheriff's department is treating it as a suicide, but I doubt it. She wasn't the type, for one thing. Maybe Lee Lee found out that Bobby wasn't going to inherit anything and took it personally. Or maybe she just realized he'd never be free, as long as his mother was alive.

Bear insists it was Pete and it was just a question of time.

About the Author

Sandra J. Robson is a speech pathologist and the author of two Keegan Shaw mysteries, *False Impression* and *False as the Day is Long*. She has lived in London and traveled extensively in the British Isles. She resides on the east coast of Florida with her orthodontist husband and is a member of Mystery Writers of America.